Secrets & Scorpions

Lorelei Gray

Foxfoot Books Paperback

This book is a work of fiction. Any references to historical events, real people, or real places are used fictitiously. Other names, characters, places, and events are products of the author's imagination, and any resemblance to actual events or places or persons, living or dead, is entirely coincidental.

Copyright © 2023 by Lorelei Gray

All rights reserved, including the right to reproduce this book or portions thereof in any form whatsoever.

Foxfoot Books first edition November 2023

Foxfoot Books and colophon are registered trademarks of Countdown Media LLC.

www.foxfootbooks.com

ISBN: 979-8-9866361-4-6

Cover design by Graphicsoul

Manufactured in the United States of America

ALSO BY LORELEI GRAY

The Black Forest Duology
Black Forest Bound
Black Forest Burning

"How terrible it would be if all my
people had been turned human by
well-meaning wizards—exiled,
trapped in burning houses."

—The Last Unicorn, Peter S. Beagle

Prologue

Long ago, there was magic in our world. Unicorns grazed in fields of ever-blooming flowers, mermaids haunted the waters, and dragon wings blocked out the sun as they soared through the skies. Things were peaceful, beautiful, balanced.

Then the humans appeared. This new species, born without magic, didn't impress the ones that had come before. The mermaids treated them like playthings, loving them and drowning them in equal measure. The dragons scorched their villages and stole their shiny objects. Unicorns refused to show themselves to any but the pure of heart, though what that meant changed like the seasons.

The witches, however, knew not to underestimate the humans. The most powerful of the magical beings, the witches knew the past, the present, the future, and the havoc these humans would one day wreak. To protect themselves, the witches left behind their natural bodies and transformed to look like humans. They chose to blend in and live among them. Watching, waiting, knowing.

Eventually the humans created their own magic in the form of weapons—and before long they had hunted all of the magical beings to near extinction. The witches watched sadly as mermaids, fairies, and even phoenixes, were murdered in droves. If they didn't step in, the humans would succeed in completely wiping out all the other magical species. So, the witches put a spell on the remaining creatures, stealing their natural forms and giving them human bodies to hide inside.

After many years of living among the humans and keeping their true identities and powers secret, the beings forgot they had ever been magical. They believed themselves to be human and forgot their own legends. The world remembered them only as myths, and all magic was lost.

Until now.

Tucson, Arizona
March

1

Three women sat at the edge of a slow river, washing bloody clothes in the water. Their bare arms were half-submerged and long dark hair obscured their faces as they bent over their work. The bloody clothes turned the river red but never seemed to get clean.

Liliana watched them from the opposite riverbank. The oppressive heat made her body feel sluggish and her thoughts muddled. She didn't know where she was or how she got there, but she couldn't take her eyes off of the three women. She heard a soft splash and the women's rhythmic washing motions ceased, their hands gripping the bloody clothes just above the waterline.

Their heads snapped up and three pairs of dark eyes landed on Liliana. Their faces were white as sun-bleached bones, with bright orange marigolds painted around each eye. Indigo tear drops decorated their cheekbones and stitched black grins stretched too far across their faces. They were beautiful--and terrifying.

The failure of the body, the first woman whispered.
The burial of the body, the second woman whispered.
The forgetting, the third woman whispered.
"The three deaths." Liliana turned to see a woman

with wavy, waist-length black hair in a flowing dress the color of clovers standing beside her.

She shivered as the woman slipped her hand into Liliana's. A cold so deep she could feel it in her blood, in her bones, seeped into her. She wanted to pull her hand out of the woman's icy grip, but had no control over her own body. She followed, powerless, as the woman led her down to the water's edge.

"The forgetting is the final death," the woman said as she gently pulled Liliana down to sit beside her at the edge of the river. "When there is no one left to remember you, only then are you truly dead." She smiled, a dazzling smile that reminded Liliana of her mother. It made her feel warm and safe, and she smiled back.

"Oh, my beautiful girl," the woman said as she gently stroked Liliana's hair. "I wanted to be forgotten. You never should have come out of the water."

A burning pain shot through her scalp as the woman clenched a fistful of her hair and forced Liliana into the river.

Coppery water filled her mouth, her lungs, as she fought against the woman's impossible strength. Liliana thrashed and clawed at the hands forcing her head down. She felt torn skin collecting underneath her fingernails, but the woman's grip did not weaken.

Just as she started to tire and give in to the water filling her lungs, a voice she had never heard before, gentle but firm, slipped into her mind.

"Abre los ojos."

2

Liliana woke up knowing someone was going to die.

The frightening dream was fading quickly, but the *feeling* of it lingered. It had taken root in the depths of her throat and was expanding—she could feel it make its way down into her chest, up into her mouth.

She stayed rigid in bed, wrapped in her blankets, and stared up at the ceiling. The old glow-in-the-dark star stickers she put up when she was a kid were still there, an ugly faded green in the dawning light. Her lemon-yellow walls glowed warmly as the sun crept over her windowsill and spilled into her room. The brightness felt wrong to her, contrasting harshly with the bitter cold she felt creeping underneath her skin. She looked around her room as if it were a stranger's. Everything—from the droopy-eyed stuffed bear her boyfriend Jeremy had given her to her book bag hanging off the back of her desk chair—felt like they belonged to someone else. Someone who didn't exist anymore.

Usually she would be out running on her regular trail by now, her skin slick with sweat and the high of adrenaline pulsing through her. But today was different. Something cold and dark was waiting outside of her bed. She could feel it all around her, even if she couldn't see it.

This wasn't how she thought she'd feel on her eighteenth birthday. She hadn't expected to feel anything, actually. She thought it would feel like any other day because that's how all her other birthdays had felt. She definitely hadn't expected to wake up with a heavy, suffocating feeling that someone was going to *die*.

Liliana cringed as she heard the familiar lilt of the *Las Mañanitas* birthday song echoing down the hall toward her room. Any minute her parents would burst in, singing—*badly*—at the top of their lungs while her little brother Mateo rolled his eyes and pretended to sing along. She knew this was going to happen because it's what happened *every* year on her birthday. She wasn't sure she would be able to fake her way through it this time.

Without bothering to knock her mother threw open her door mid-verse, causing the full-length mirror hanging on the back of the door to shudder. Her mother raised her arms above her head dramatically as she neared the end of the song.

"... *Despierta, Liliana, despierta, mira que ya amaneció, ya los parajillos cantan, la luna ya se metió!*

Liliana's father and brother were close behind, as were her mother's three little fluffy black Pomeranians—or as her father called them, the *hell hounds*. Their tiny nails clicked against the ceramic tile floor as they raced into her room. She smiled weakly and sat up in bed, reaching out her arms to receive them. Their excited wiggles and incessant kisses always cheered her up. But instead of jumping onto her bed and into her arms like they usually did, they stopped in the middle of the room, a few feet away from her. They stopped so abruptly that Tonto, their tripod Pomeranian, slid across the tile floor and disappeared underneath her bed. In a second he was back in sight, sitting beside his brothers. The three dogs sat shoulder to shoulder, staring up at her, their tiny heads tilting one way, then the other, as if they didn't recognize her. Liliana's face fell and she let her arms drop to her sides.

"What are they doing?" Mateo said, still in his pajamas, cartoon cats grinning at her from his shirt. His dark, wavy hair stuck up in every direction and a long indentation across one of his baby-fat cheeks told her he'd fallen asleep on top of a book again last night.

"*Tus perritos locos.*" Her mother directed at the dogs, shaking her head as she scooped up Gordito, the plumpest of the three poms. She gave the dog an affectionate little squeeze and sat down on the bed next to Liliana. The chunky Pomeranian squirmed in her mother's arms until she relented and set the dog back on the floor. He rejoined his brothers and they remained where they were, sitting, uncharacteristically calm, a few feet away from her bed.

Liliana dragged her gaze off the little dogs to look at her mother. Violeta Presagio-Jones had one of those faces other people's moms were jealous of. Flawless skin, full smiling lips, and heavily lashed dark-brown eyes that seemed to see everything, things no one else could see. She was practically Liliana's twin—except her mother's long dark hair was spider webbed with silver. A bright grin spread across her mother's face and she scooped Liliana, covers and all, into her arms. The smell of white sage and turpentine suffocated her as she pressed her wine-red lips repeatedly to Liliana's face.

Liliana squirmed in the straitjacket the blankets had become and tried to pull away from her mother's incessant kisses. No use, though, she knew. One kiss for every year she'd been alive—it was one of the many birthday traditions her mother forced upon her and her brother. It was better if she just accepted it. She knew from experience if she fought her mother would "lose count" and start all over.

Finally, the onslaught ceased, and she squirmed out of her mother's grasp like Gordito had.

"Oh, you know you're going to miss my kisses when you go off to college, *ya verás*!"

"I doubt it," Liliana grumbled as she wiped at the dark-red lipstick smears her mother left on her cheeks. Liliana recently received her acceptance letter to her first-choice school. It was on the East Coast, miles away from her family, from her friends, from everything she had ever known. Her family would always be part of her, but she wanted something that was entirely hers. A life she designed for herself instead of the life her parents had formed for her.

She looked over at her dad who stood a few feet away. David Jones had developed a bit of a belly, only accentuated by the faded blue T-shirt he wore tucked into his jeans. His grain-colored hair was barely touched with gray and his face was always a little sunburned from working outside. He was holding up his phone, pointed directly at Liliana.

"*Dios mío*, are you filming this?" Horrified, she threw one of her pillows at him. It fell short, surprising the dogs and causing them to scatter out of the room.

"Of course," he said, lowering his phone to meet his daughter's eyes, "we have to capture your eighteenth birthday! You'll thank me when you're old and want to remember the good ol' days." He held his phone back up.

For those first few minutes everything had felt normal. Annoying, but normal. The dark feeling she'd woken up with pushed away to the edges. She should have known it wasn't going to last. The tickle in her throat was now a painful throbbing, and she struggled to swallow.

Her hands flew to her neck, urgently exploring her throat with her fingers. Her lymph nodes weren't swollen, yet her throat felt itchy and thick. *No en mi cumpleaños*, she thought miserably. She couldn't believe she was getting sick on her birthday. She didn't want to miss school, and her boyfriend was going to take her out to dinner ...

Her father watched her with a slight look of concern pinching his thick, blond eyebrows together. He lowered his phone to his side.

"Are you alright, honey?" her father asked, coming closer to her. She lowered her hands and let them drop into her lap.

"I—" she choked out with difficulty, "I think I'm sick."

"Are we done?" Mateo whined, arms crossed as he leaned against the door frame. His mouth twisted into an annoyed scowl. "I'm hungry."

Liliana's mother *tisked* and shook her head at Mateo. "You better be nice to your sister, Mateo, or El Coco will come get you tonight!"

Mateo rolled his eyes. "I don't believe in the boogeyman anymore, Mamá. *Ya no soy un bebé.*"

Her mother scoffed and waved him out of the room.

"My throat really hurts," Liliana said as softly as she could to avoid hurting her throat even more.

Her mother frowned and raised a hand streaked with dried orange paint to rest on her forehead. A moment passed, two. Her mother closed her eyes as if that would help her take a more accurate temperature. Her father disappeared and reappeared just as quickly, a digital thermometer in his hand. She was relieved to see it was the human one, and not the large livestock thermometer he sometimes brought out as a joke. A *not funny* joke that seemed to bring him no end of amusement. When she was younger, she used to laugh hysterically at her father's antics—her favorite was when he pretended he was looking for something in his veterinary bag, always something that would never be there. Liliana's missing shoe, one of the dogs, a birthday cake. But she wasn't a little kid anymore.

"Here you go, hon," her dad said as he held the thermometer out to Liliana. Her mother's hand dropped from her forehead.

"I'm the only ther*mom*eter she needs," her mother rebuked, the familiar joke eliciting nothing but groans from Liliana. She took the thermometer from her father's outstretched hand and placed it underneath her tongue. She closed her mouth around the instrument and waited uncomfortably for the device to beep. Her dad loomed over them, his clear blue eyes darkening with worry. Her mother attempted to smooth Liliana's wild bedhead hair down but quickly gave up. They waited awkwardly in silence until finally the thermometer beeped three times. She took it out of her mouth and looked at the numbers displayed: 98.6 degrees. Normal.

Her mother snatched the thermometer from her hand and glanced at it before handing it back to Liliana's father. She leaned in close and whispered, "See, now if you had just used your ther*mom*eter maybe I sense a fever, now too bad, you have to go to school."

"Lili, hon, if you're not feeling well you can stay home," her father said. Usually it'd take immense blood loss or projectile vomiting for him to allow her or her brother to stay home from school. She raised an eyebrow at him.

He leaned down and planted a firm kiss on top of her head. "Happy birthday."

Liliana managed a weak smile and raised a hand to rest on her warm, aching throat. No fever, no symptoms aside from the sudden sore throat and a deep certainty of impending doom.

What's wrong with me?

Her parents finally left her alone to get dressed but she remained stuck to her bed, filled with a confusing mixture of dread and determination. Something was very *not right* with her, but she didn't want to miss school. Not on her *birthday*. And she had track practice after school, and her dinner with Jeremy.

Her throat burned and an anxiety she'd never felt before rushed through her, making her hands shake. She eyed the outfit she'd picked out the night before, a sand-colored linen romper that was comfortable and airy but also hugged her curves in just the right way. She pushed through the dark feelings, her aching throat, and got dressed, pulling on a matching pair of chunky espadrille sandals. They accentuated her strong, muscled calves she'd developed running track for the last three years.

She gave herself a once-over in the full-length mirror hanging off the back of her door. She considered her long, wavy hair. Usually she'd pull it back into a ponytail or weave it into a long braid, but today she let it run wild down her back.

Grabbing her book bag off her desk, she shoved a few textbooks inside and her copy of *Wuthering Heights*, a book she was supposed to be reading for English class but hadn't made it past the first chapter. She snatched her car keys from her desk and tossed them into the bag with her cell phone.

No matter how hard she tried to focus on these normal, everyday tasks, she couldn't ignore the dark feeling lingering inside of her since waking up. It was still there, heavy in her chest, her lungs.

Someone is going to die.

She tried to shake out the dark thought crowding her brain. Her rational self knew this was all crazy. How could she know something like that? But also, *of course* someone was going to die. People die all the time.

She grabbed her sagebrush green school sweatshirt, with Ventana High's coyote mascot grinning from the front, and stuffed it into the bag, too. No matter how hot it got outside, the air conditioning kept the classrooms freezing.

Walking down the hall, she passed her brother's room and the bathroom they shared, into the kitchen where the smell of coffee and eggs intermingled. The kitchen's large windows let in the morning light, and for the millionth time in her life, she admired the view of the hills and distant saguaros. She was excited to leave Tucson for college, but she was going to miss the desert. She had considered staying and attending the University of Arizona like most of her friends, but she didn't even apply. If she applied, and she got in, the temptation to stay would be too strong. She wasn't sure she wouldn't succumb to it. Staying at home would be cheaper; she would already have friends at school, everything, she knew, would be easier if she stayed in Tucson for college. Everything, she knew, would stay the same.

Liliana wanted to push herself, force herself out of her comfort zone and find out who she was away from everything she'd ever known. She'd mapped out her future and turned it into a long checklist of tasks. "Get into college" was already checked off—she'd be moving to the East Coast in the fall to study architectural engineering. She wasn't entirely sure she wouldn't change majors, but she always loved math, the certainty of numbers. In math there was always a right answer.

Her father was at the kitchen counter pouring

coffee into his scratched-up travel mug. He dumped a disgusting amount of sugar into the coffee then screwed on the lid. Her brother had changed into his school clothes and was sitting at the kitchen table, slowly forking huevos rancheros into his mouth as he read one of his books. He'd recently been experimenting with hair gel and she smirked at his slicked back hair. Liliana tousled it as she walked past then immediately regretted it, her hand sticky with gel.

"*¿Por que?*" he whined, glaring at her as he tried to smooth his hair back into place.

Liliana shrugged. "Why not?"

Mateo glowered at her and went back to his book. She considered doing it again—just to *really* annoy him—but washed the stickiness of the hair gel off her hand instead and left him to his reading.

Liliana glanced around the kitchen and peeked into the formal dining room they rarely used but didn't see her mother.

"Where's mom?"

"Where else?" her dad said as he nodded toward the backyard where her mother's art studio sat.

Liliana nodded; she didn't know why she had bothered to ask. If her mother wasn't hovering around her or her brother, she was out in her studio painting. Her work was sold in a few galleries downtown and a couple up in Phoenix. She painted beautiful desert landscapes in bright, cheerful colors. She also did paintings of local animals—herds of javelinas, howling coyotes, jewel-winged hummingbirds. Tourists loved that shit.

"She made breakfast for you." Her dad gestured at a plate covered in tinfoil. She peeled off the foil and quickly ate her own portion of huevos rancheros standing at the counter.

"Are you feeling better?" her dad asked, his pale blue eyes searching her own for answers she couldn't give. She swallowed her last bite down and nodded. *This is nothing,* she told herself. *Probably just a combination of allergies and that awful nightmare I had.*

"Okay, if you're sure." Her dad he patted her on the arm. "Your eyes look dark, maybe you just didn't get enough sleep."

"Sure, that's probably it."

Her father's cell phone rang, an overly jarring sound.

"Hello?" he answered. Liliana and Mateo watched him, waiting for the bad news. It was never good when his cell phone rang this early in the morning.

"Yes, I'll be right over. Keep applying pressure." He hung up with a pained sigh and looked at his two children who stared back at him with question marks in their eyes.

"Another livestock attack," he said as he grabbed his veterinary bag out of the hall closet. He paused at the entryway console table and scooped his car keys out of the official "keys dish"—an ugly clay bowl that was supposed to resemble a lemon her mother made during a, thankfully, brief pottery phase.

Liliana frowned. Her father had been tending to a slew of farm animals, mostly goats, being attacked in the area. There had been at least one a week for the last month or so. In all cases, he'd been unable to save the animals.

He turned back to Liliana and gave her his classic *I'm sorry* smile. "Happy birthday, honey. I'll see you later tonight."

An unfamiliar ache bloomed in her chest as we watched him leave. A wild thought raced through her mind. *What if this is the last time I see him?*

She shook the thought away and picked up her school bag. She just needed to get out of the house and go to school. *Things will be normal at school. They have to be.*

"Liliana!" Her mother called from the backyard. Liliana could see her through the sliding glass door, standing in front of her art studio.

Liliana groaned and checked the time on her phone. She could spare about two minutes before she was set off schedule. She slid the glass door open and rolled it shut behind her.

"What?"

Her mother gestured for Liliana to follow her and dashed inside her art studio. The studio was a small earth-toned building with rounded corners and thick stucco walls. Her mother wanted complete privacy, so it was built without windows, but with skylights on the roof to let in natural light. Liliana stepped into the studio and cringed. It was always messy, but today it was particularly bad. Half-used paint tubes scattered on the floor, and paintbrushes with pointy, hardened bristles from not being washed filled dusty mason jars. Canvases in all shapes and sizes leaned against the walls and half-finished pieces sat on easels. Her mother never worked on one painting at a time, she liked to move back and forth between different projects. The chemical stench of wet oil paint filled the room and was already starting to give Liliana a headache. She wondered how her mother survived breathing in the fumes all day long.

"I wanted to show you your birthday present before you left," her mother said as she led Liliana down a goat path through the mess to a large rectangular canvas sitting vertically on an easel in the back of the room. "It's still wet, so don't touch it."

Liliana swallowed as she stared at the painting. Her own dark, intense eyes stared back at her. It was a portrait of herself, standing in the desert at dawn, looking out at the viewer. Her mother rarely painted people, but when she did, they always had this creepy quality to them. Like they were alive, watching, trapped inside the painting.

A small fox was in the background; its amber eyes locked onto the Liliana in the painting. She had never seen her mother paint a fox before. It was usually coyotes, birds, rabbits, and sometimes the three Pomeranians.

"I saw the fox in a dream," her mother said, as if reading her mind. "It was such a surreal dream, the fox felt ... it felt like he had a message." Liliana slid her eyes from the painting to her mother. Her mother looked back at her and laughed. "*¡No sé!*"

Liliana's mother had never talked about dreams before; she didn't believe in "woo-woo stuff," as she called it. Of all the strange things that happened that morning, this might actually be the strangest.

"*¿Te gusta la pintura?*" her mother asked, a touch of

worry in her voice.

Liliana looked back at the painting. Other kids got iPhones or laptops or a new car for their eighteenth birthday; she got a painting. She forced a smile onto her face.

"Of course I like it, Mamá!" Liliana gave her a quick hug. "*Muchas gracias.*"

Her mother looked at her suspiciously for a moment, then smiled back.

"Are you going to be home for dinner?" her mother asked as she turned away from the painting. She pressed Liliana lightly on the back to urge her forward and out of the studio.

"No, Jeremy is taking me out to dinner for my birthday, remember?"

"Mm, right."

Liliana rolled her eyes; she'd told her about it multiple times. It shouldn't matter, the real party—the big family birthday party her mother was throwing Liliana—was on Saturday. She cringed internally, remembering how over the top her *quinceañera* had been. Her mother had been very secretive about the party, which only made Liliana *more* nervous. *At least I won't have to wear a poofy dress this time.*

"*Bueno*, well save some room for dessert. I'm going to make you your favorite."

Liliana smiled. Her "favorite" was just warm peaches with cinnamon on top of ice cream. Her mother was an amazing cook, but a truly awful baker. Over the years, she'd tried to bake all kinds of cakes and cookies, and every time it turned out inedible. She'd use baking soda instead of baking powder, or cook it too long, or leave an ingredient out entirely if she didn't have it on hand. A couple years ago, Liliana told her mother her favorite dessert was peaches and ice cream because it was something she knew her mother could actually make.

"Thank you, Mami. I have to go. I'm going to be late picking up Ava." She pressed a kiss to her mother's soft cheek.

"Go, go, I'll see you later," her mother waved her off and turned to go back into her studio.

Liliana walked toward the sliding glass door and paused. "Don't forget you're taking Mateo to school today!" she called back to her mother.

Her mother slapped herself on the forehead and turned around, away from her studio. "What am I going to do without you when you're gone?" she moaned. "Your brother will just never go to school I guess."

3

Liliana let the screen door slap shut behind her as she left the house. The air outside was already heating up, the sky a faded, cloudless blue. She took the few short steps down from the porch, then froze at the top of the driveway when she saw it. The sedan, usually a dirt-specked forest green, was now coated in shining black feathers.

Crows covered her car from the hood to the taillights. Their feathers had a greasy, bluish sheen and their sharp, focused eyes locked onto her. They were all staring at her—every single one.

A couple of the large birds flapped their wings, as if trying to get comfortable on the hard body of her car, but most were perfectly still.

She took another step forward, but the crows didn't move.

"Um, go away!" she yelled, her voice weaker than she had planned it to be. She held tightly to the strap of her tote bag with one hand and waved at the crows with her other. They remained motionless. "Get off my car!"

The birds practically yawned at her, stretching out their wings, then folding them back against their bodies. She knew crows to be stubborn, to wait until the very last second to move out of the road when a car was coming, or to work at a trashcan lid for hours until it fell open to reveal the scavenger delicacies within. But this ...

She looked around and picked up a small rock, considering. Her aim wouldn't be good enough, she decided. With her luck, she'd end up throwing it right through the windshield.

A pickup truck roared down the street and she turned. Music blasted from the inside of the massive vehicle, and she felt the deep base in her bones, in her teeth.

The truck slowed to a stop in front of her house and let out a long, blaring honk. The crows alighted at the sound, filling the air around her with flapping wings and shimmering feathers. She let out an involuntary scream and raised her arms to cover her face, but none of the birds touched her. When she lowered her arms, the crows were gone.

Finn Collins, another senior at her school, rolled the truck's driver side window down. He leaned out and flashed her his trademark mischievous grin. His thick, pumpkin-orange hair was cut short on the sides and left longer on top. His face heavily freckled and slightly sunburned except for a pale outline of sunglasses around his eyes. Helsie, his on-again-off-again girlfriend, was in the passenger's seat. She leaned over him, her long, curly blonde hair spilling across Finn's face as she waved at Liliana.

"Hey, girl, heeeeey!" Helsie called out in her foreign,

Mississippi-sweet accent. Her bright-blue eyes outlined a little too darkly in black eyeliner, and her lips glittered with bright pink lip gloss.

"Hey, Helsie," Liliana called back weakly, still shaken from the crow's sudden flight.

Finn pushed Helsie gently back into her seat and jerked his head toward Liliana's car.

"That was nuts! I've never seen so many crows at once before. What'd you do, cover your car with bird seed?"

"Ha, ha," Liliana said as she rolled her eyes.

"You coming to the game on Friday?"

Liliana shrugged. Her cousin Diego was on the baseball team with Finn and the whole family would usually go to watch his games. She wasn't sure if they would go to this one, with all the planning that needed to happen for her birthday party the next day.

"Alrighty, see you in class," he called as he revved the engine and sped off.

Liliana watched Finn's ridiculous truck disappear down the street and tried to shake off the weirdness of the morning as she slid into her car. She set her book bag down on the passenger seat and took a deep breath of the warming rosemary scent coming from the little muslin bag hanging from her rearview mirror. Her friend Ruby had made a different sachet for everyone in their group, each holding a specific herb for each person. Ruby told Liliana hers was filled with rosemary to help her "focus on the road." It was sort of a joke, and sort of wasn't. Liliana wasn't a *bad* driver, but she did zone out a lot. She was notorious for missing turns and exits and forgetting to pay attention to her navigation app.

She reached up and gave the little bag a pinch to amplify the scent. Her hand froze halfway back to the steering wheel when something black and shiny caught her eye through the windshield: the crows. They hadn't left when Finn honked, only moved to the giant walnut tree that grew in the front yard.

Liliana pulled out of her driveway a little faster than usual. She turned and drove the same direction Finn had gone—toward the school. Instead of heading straight for campus, though, she turned off the main road and down a wide residential street much like her own. Every house was a different shade of beige, or brown, or white. The tidy front yards included various configurations of rocks and cacti, low-maintenance and low-water landscaping.

She neared Ava's familiar creamy-white stucco house with a family of five cut-metal coyotes decorating the yard, their noses pointed toward the sky in a perpetual howl. Liliana had been pulling up to this house her whole life, but more often recently as she was Ava's ride to school most days. Ava was forced to rely on Liliana, their other friends, and her parents for rides after she totaled her own car after a party a little over a month ago. She had swerved to avoid hitting a hare that hopped in front of her car and ran right into a giant saguaro cactus. Her parents had a one-strike policy, so she didn't get another car.

Ava was already outside, waiting at the bottom of her driveway for her. She wore her black-framed glasses and her chin-length dark hair looked like it was still damp from her morning shower. She was sporting her favorite pair of beaten-up sneakers with cut-off jean shorts and a loose-fitting black T-shirt with "Green Light" scrawled across the front in vibrant, neon-green lettering. Liliana remembered when she got that shirt. Ava made her wait with her in the painfully long merch line when the band played in Tucson last year. Ava refused to admit it, but she was a little obsessed with the lead singer, a gorgeous blond guy with a striking voice and only one hand.

Ava was scowling as she opened the passenger side door and dropped heavily down into the seat, her fraying black backpack in her lap.

"You're late," she grumbled, then made a face. "Ugh, what's that smell?"

"What smell?" Liliana sniffed but all she could smell was the rosemary hanging from her mirror. She pointed to the bundle of herbs. "Is it the rosemary?"

Ava leaned forward and sniffed, an odd expression flashing across her face. She sat back and shrugged. "Must be." Ava pulled a square plastic container from her backpack and dropped it into Liliana's lap. "Here. Happy birthday." Liliana picked it up and admired the sopapillas inside—the golden-brown pillows of fried dough glistened with some sort of syrup.

"The syrup is just wildflower honey. I didn't have time to make anything special—"

"You're the best!" Liliana grinned, leaning awkwardly over the console to give Ava a half-hug. Ava was a master at making desserts and she knew sopapillas were Liliana's *real* favorite. Just seeing the sopapillas chased away the dark thoughts of the morning and she was relieved *something* good had happened. She shyly opened the container and plucked out one of the little fried dough pillows. She took a bite and closed her eyes in pleasure. Crunchy, soft, sweet, sticky—*perfect*. She chewed and swallowed and gave Ava an appreciative smile. "Oh my God, that was amazing." She licked the stickiness of the honey from her fingertips.

"Thanks," Ava smirked. "You'll have to hide them or Ruby will eat them all."

"Oh, I *know*." Their friend Ruby had a notorious sweet tooth, but her parents thought white sugar was poison so she had to get her sweets in secret. That usually meant pilfering treats from her friends.

"Can you put them in my bag for me?" She put the lid back on the container and handed it to Ava, who slipped it into Liliana's tote bag on the floor.

She pulled away from Ava's house and continued driving down the street toward their school. Cookie-cutter houses made way for strip malls and gas stations. She gritted her teeth as the car hit a pothole she had failed to avoid.

"So, do you feel any different? Being eighteen?" Ava asked as she tapped something into her phone.

Do I feel any different? Liliana wasn't sure how to answer that.

"Ah, well, something weird did happen this morning, it's why I was late picking you up, actually." Liliana wasn't ready to admit that she was suffering from an inexplicable sore throat, or that she woke up with a strong feeling that someone was going to die, but the *crows* she could talk about. She at least knew the crows were real since Finn and Helsie saw them, too.

"Oh?" Ava looked up from her phone. "What happened?"

"Well, when I went outside to get into my car there were, like, a hundred crows on it."

"A murder," Ava said simply.

"What?" Liliana's heart beat faster at the word. *Someone is going to die.* Her throat grew hot and ached; she tried to swallow the feeling down.

"That's what a group of crows are called, a *murder of crows.*"

"*Por supuesto.* A *murder*? Why is that what a group of crows is called?"

Ava shrugged. "Collective nouns for birds is so interesting. A *paddling* of ducks, a *mob* of emus, a *charm* of finches. A group of starlings is called a murmuring—how poetic is that?"

Liliana side-eyed her friend. "Why do you know so much about what groups of birds are called?"

Ava shrugged again. "Had to look up what a group of quails is called for a paper I was writing, a *bevy*, by the way, and it sort of snowballed from there."

Liliana smiled and shook her head, amused. "Okay weirdo, well a *murder* of crows was on my car. And you're going to think I'm crazy, but I swear they were all ... *staring* at me."

Liliana slowed to stop at a red light and turned to Ava, who was looking back at her from behind her lightly scratched glasses.

"Well of course they were staring at you," Ava said as she looked back down at her phone. "You were staring at *them*, weren't you?"

"Well ... yeah, I mean, I guess—"

"Crows are incredibly smart creatures. They can remember faces, and they hold grudges. You didn't do anything to piss them off, did you?"

Liliana jumped as the car behind them blasted their horn. The light had turned green and she hadn't been paying attention. She gave the bag of rosemary an accusatory glare as she stepped on the gas pedal.

"I don't think so," she answered once they'd cleared the intersection. "But they probably aren't big fans of Finn, he pulled up in that giant truck of his and honked at them."

"Oh, he's screwed. They're going to follow him and shit all over his truck."

Liliana let out a short laugh and couldn't help but smirk at the image of Finn's prized truck covered in crow crap.

"You laugh," Ava said in a warning tone, one eyebrow raised, "but wait and see. They will get their revenge."

Liliana's smile faded away as she remembered how coldly the birds had studied her. How their sharp eyes followed her as she moved, how they were probably still waiting for her in the branches of the walnut tree.

"Liliana!"

She jumped and snapped her head to look at Ava, who peered at her with worried eyes.

"What?" Liliana looked around, nothing had happened, she was still driving, on autopilot, toward school.

"You looked like you were a million miles away and completely ignoring me. Are you okay?"

Liliana tried to remember the last thing Ava said—something about revenge. Had she said more than that? Liliana hated that she didn't know.

"Gifts," Ava said. "I was saying that crows like gifts. They like to get them and to give them. If you leave something out for them, they might bring you something back in return."

"Like what?" Liliana asked, though she had no intention of doing anything to encourage the crows to stick around.

"Well, people often leave out bowls of water for them, or food. They might bring you a candy wrapper, a paperclip, other shiny things."

"So, trash?"

Ava shrugged. "I'm just saying, it's better to have crows on your side. Don't piss them off. One time my dad waved a crow off one of the patio chairs and for the next month it dive-bombed him every time he left the house. I thought it was hysterical, of course, but he didn't think so."

Liliana smiled as she imagined Mr. Lopez ducking and weaving to avoid a vengeful crow. Her smile faded as she imagined herself in his place. If those crows were still there when she came home from school ... she shook the thought away.

Liliana turned her car into the senior parking lot. No one monitored who parked there, but there was a general understanding that it was reserved for seniors. It was the lot closest to the school, seniority earning them a shorter walk to class and not much else.

She parked the car and walked with Ava toward their

lockers, which were next to each other. Ava's assigned locker was in a different building entirely, but she'd convinced one of their classmates to switch with her so she could be by Liliana's.

The classrooms were built in a semicircle around a large open-air space they all referred to as "the quad" with the massive gym looming on the other side. When it wasn't roasting hot out, she and her friends would eat outside in the open space, but they usually ended up in the air-conditioned cafeteria with everyone else.

Ava hit her locker door with the side of her fist, and it popped open. She'd learned this trick when she took over the locker from their classmate freshman year—it was locked unless you hit it in just the right spot. Ava never even bothered putting a combination lock on it like the rest of them had to.

Liliana spun her own necessary lock back and forth until it clicked open. She pulled the textbooks she wouldn't need until after lunch out of her tote bag but held onto her unread copy of *Wuthering Heights* and her environmental science textbook for her first classes.

She paused when she saw the container of sopapillas in her bag. Ava wasn't joking about Ruby eating them all if she saw them. She guiltily stuffed her sweatshirt on top, hiding the sopapillas from view.

A pair of strong arms wrapped around her waist from behind and she stumbled as she was pulled against a warm body. She looked down at the arms around her and immediately recognized the tanned skin, the constellation of five moles on his left arm.

"Happy birthday, beautiful," a soft voice whispered

in her ear. It sent shivers through her and she twisted around in her boyfriend's arms to look up at him. Jeremy smiled with the air of confidence he always had, relaxed, but always in control. His slightly overgrown hair was the color of burnt honey and fell over his dark-blue eyes as he looked down at her. She enjoyed the comfortable fit of his body against hers and closed her eyes as he leaned down to kiss her. Their mouths met and her heart beat a little faster the way it always did when Jeremy kissed her.

"Later," Ava grunted from behind her. Liliana pulled back from Jeremy and turned to see Ava already walking away, her head bent as she focused on something on her phone.

"Bye!" Liliana yelled, louder than she needed to, just to annoy Ava. A pair of freshman girls walking past looked at her with wide, frightened eyes. Ava waved without looking back.

Jeremy pulled her back against his body but she resisted.

"I have to get to class," she whined.

Jeremy gave her an exaggerated pout then reached into his pocket. He pulled out a small box wrapped in silvery paper and offered it to her.

Liliana forgot about being late to class and eagerly took the present from Jeremy. She began to slide her finger under the edge of the wrapping paper to open it, but he stopped her.

"No, not yet," he said, wagging a finger at her. "You have to wait until tonight to open it."

"Then why did you give it to me now?" she groaned.

She held the small box up to her ear and gave it a gentle shake, but she couldn't hear anything rattle inside. Liliana put the puzzle together quickly in her mind—small box, no sound. Jewelry was often sold between layers of soft, sound-blocking cotton. She was certain it was jewelry, but couldn't tell by the size if it was earrings, or a necklace, or a bracelet ...

Jeremy plucked the small box back from her and she frowned.

"I don't think I can trust you to not open it until tonight," Jeremy said, smirking. "I'll hang on to it for you until later."

She eyed the little silver box in his hand. He was probably right—she wouldn't make it past first period without opening it.

"Fine," she said begrudgingly.

Jeremy leaned over and gave her a quick kiss.

"I have to go before I'm late to class," she turned and walked a few steps away from him, then turned back to call out, "Don't lose my present!"

Jeremy smiled and shook his head before going the opposite direction to his own first period class.

Hurrying past the first two buildings, she paused before entering the third where her English class was held. An odd feeling crept across her skin, and she had the distinct impression someone was watching her. She hesitated, a little afraid of what she would see when she turned around. Another murder of crows? Something worse?

Liliana turned and swept her eyes over the emptying courtyard. A towering black willow tree on the other side of the quad swayed gently in the low breeze, its dark bark a spindly shadow against the red-bricked science building behind it. Near the base of the tree, in the shadows, she saw a small flash of dark red, the glint of amber eyes. She blinked and there was nothing there, just wood chips and a few pieces of trash.

She tried to laugh at herself but it was difficult. She must have imagined it, the weirdness of the morning was leaking into her mind, confusing her, making her see things that weren't there.

I'm losing it, she thought. *I'm really losing it.*

4

Liliana slid into her assigned seat one row from the back of Mrs. Crane's English class moments before the second bell rang. She pulled out her copy of *Wuthering Heights* and stared at it. The cover featured a woman's silhouette looking out a window into a dark night. She thought it was going to be a creepy ghost story, but when she got to the second chapter, it was like any boring old-timey love story. She tried to read the book, she really had, but it put her to sleep. Since she was pretty certain Mrs. Crane didn't read their papers anyway and she'd already been accepted to college, she wondered what the point was.

Mrs. Crane puttered into the classroom, looking a little more frazzled than usual. Her graying brown hair was pulled up into a clip, but long strands slipped out around her sun-wrinkled face. Her skin had a slight sheen to it, as if she'd run to class.

The teacher set her satchel down on top of her cluttered desk and looked out at them. Some of the others were still chatting, oblivious or intentionally ignoring Mrs. Crane waiting for them to stop. Liliana didn't have any friends in this class. If she did, she'd probably be chatting away, too. Instead she sat quietly, watching Mrs. Crane watch them.

The English teacher's voice rose warily over the hum of the student chatter, asking everyone to settle down, be quiet, get to your seats.

Liliana stared down at the book in front of her and picked at the edge of the paperback's cover, absentmindedly pulling apart a corner. Her throat was throbbing again, and she wondered if she had strep throat.

She thought about the amber eyes glowing within the hanging branches of the willow tree. Were they really just a trick of the eye? A reflection of discarded candy wrappers? She couldn't shake the feeling of being watched. First by the crows, then by some unknown entity in the courtyard. *It's all in your head,* she told herself firmly.

"Liliana, you shared such good insight about Daisy Buchanan when we read *The Great Gatsby*, what do you think about Catherine's character?"

At the sound of her name, Liliana's focus shattered, and she looked up to see Mrs. Crane staring at her. Waiting for, it seemed, an intelligent and thoughtful response to her question.

"Er ..." Liliana glanced around at the other students surrounding her but most of them weren't paying attention and those who were looked bored. Isabel, the girl sitting in front of her, turned slightly and mouthed something she couldn't understand.

Catherine?

Liliana looked down at the book at the woman on the

cover. *Is that Catherine? Shit.*

"I ... uh ... no."

Mrs. Crane tilted her head and looked at Liliana with disappointment, then turned away, continuing the lecture on the book's characters and their motivations. Liliana's face felt warm as she slid down in her chair. The look of disappointment on Mrs. Crane's face stung worse than it should have. *Why didn't I just read the stupid book?*

Liliana stayed like that, slumped down in her chair, hiding behind her long, wavy hair, while the rest of the class debated plot points and character development Liliana knew nothing about. When the bell finally rang, she grabbed her bag and slipped out of the classroom before Mrs. Crane had a chance to stop her. She glanced around and, when she didn't see anyone she knew nearby, slipped a sopapilla out of the container hidden in her bag and stuffed it into her mouth. There were only three left, and while she did want to save them, she couldn't bring them home with her. She didn't want to hurt her mom's feelings.

She felt a hand on her arm and winced. Liliana turned around prepared to suffer Mrs. Crane's wrath but was surprised to see that it was Isabel instead. Isabel's dark, stick-straight hair barely dusted her shoulders and her big eyes—really *too big*, Liliana thought—looked at her with an odd desperation Liliana didn't understand. Her throat started to hurt again, swelling up so much she couldn't swallow. It hurt to speak and she desperately wanted some water to wash the sopapilla down and soothe her throat.

"What?" she gasped out, hoping that was sufficient.

"Sorry about earlier," Isabel said, an annoying pull to her voice. She chewed on her bottom lip and clutched at the straps of her backpack. Liliana grimaced at Isabel's nails. They'd been chewed down past the flesh of her fingers, her cuticles inflamed and ragged. Isabel looked at her with wide, glossy eyes.

"What?" Liliana repeated, glancing toward the science building on the other side of campus where she should be.

"I tried to help you, with the question, but I didn't know how to tell you, and—"

Liliana waved the girl's words away. "It's fine," Liliana choked out, her throat painfully sore.

Isabel was always in the periphery, and Liliana couldn't remember the last time she'd spoken to her. She was quiet, didn't have many friends, and was usually attached to her boyfriend, Ben. She stared back at Isabel, wondering what it was she wanted from her. Liliana had the odd urge to pat her on the head.

She was going to be late to her environmental science class if she didn't go now. She waved at Isabel, hoping that sufficed as a goodbye. As she walked away, Liliana had the uncomfortable sense that she hurt Isabel's feelings. She struggled to understand how Isabel's feelings had become *her* problem, just because she didn't answer a question in class. *So annoying.*

Liliana sped across campus, through the courtyard, and toward the science building. Other students spilled into the courtyard from every direction, brushing past her as she moved against the current of bodies.

As she approached the red-brick science building, she slowed. The black willow tree stationed in front swayed gently in the soft breeze, and Liliana shivered recalling the feeling of being watched. As she passed the tree something floating in the air made her pause. A butterfly with garnet wings edged in gold drifted and bobbed toward her. She watched, mesmerized, as the creature landed on her bare shoulder. She held her breath and tried to stay still as it slowly bat its wings. Her throat felt better, she realized, as she watched the butterfly. Still a little sore, but nothing like it had been a minute ago.

She admired the colorful wings and imagined a butterfly tattoo on her shoulder where the insect currently rested. Now that she was eighteen, she could finally get a tattoo. She'd been thinking about it ever since she'd gone with Ava when she got hers, but hadn't decided on anything yet. She wanted the tattoo to mean something, but she also wanted it to be pretty. She'd struggled to come up with anything that was both meaningful *and* pretty. For a second she wondered if this experience counted as meaningful.

A presence, tall and shadowy, came up behind her.

"That's a mourning cloak butterfly you got there," said a gentle voice she recognized as her science teacher. She turned to glance at him, careful not to disturb the butterfly resting on her shoulder. Mr. Henderson was lanky with thinning blond hair and hideous gold wire-framed glasses that looked like they belonged on someone twice his age. He wore a white lab coat with coffee stains down the front over a blue button-up shirt.

His tie was covered with drawings of squiggly little creatures Liliana guessed were supposed to be some sort of bacterium.

Mourning cloak butterfly? The dark feeling from that morning pushed forward.

"Black willow trees are one of their many host plants, so we get them over here every year. We're nearing their mating season, actually," he continued, ignoring her lack of a response. "Looks like this one is a little early. Probably a male, staked out on your shoulder looking for a mate."

"Ew!" She waved the butterfly away and mentally trashed the tattoo idea. She suddenly felt stupid, trying to force meaning onto what turned out to be just a horny butterfly. It floated away and disappeared into the willow's long hanging branches. Mr. Henderson chuckled and shrugged his bony shoulders. He continued toward the classroom but she hesitated, watching the dripping willow branches shift in the soft breeze.

* * *

Liliana absentmindedly teetered back and forth on her lopsided lab stool. She stared at the blank wall-to-wall whiteboard at the front of the class, ghosts of past lectures vaguely visible even after being erased. At the front of the room Mr. Henderson explained the experiment for the day, but she wasn't paying attention. She thought about the black willow tree and the amber eyes she thought she had seen that morning. The feeling of being watched clung to her like a wet shirt.

She sensed a sudden shift in the energy of the room

and looked around. Mr. Henderson had stopped talking and was now sitting at his computer, typing away. Everyone else was pulling out microscopes from the cabinets and returning to their lab tables. Killian, her assigned lab partner for that semester, glared at her over the microscope he must have brought back to their table while she was zoning out.

Killian had dyed black hair and flour-pale skin with a scattering of bright red acne across his forehead and cheekbones. He was usually hunched over a notebook, scribbling or drawing, and spoke mostly in scowls. He smelled strongly of musty clothes and unwashed dogs. Liliana tried to be nice to him but he made it difficult.

"Sorry, I missed what Mr. Henderson said, what are we doing?" She glanced around at the other tables for clues.

Killian sighed dramatically and rolled his eyes. "Face mites."

Liliana blinked at him, uncertain if he was telling the truth or messing with her.

"I'm sorry, what now?"

"Face. Mites." Killian repeated and gestured at the board. She turned to see Mr. Henderson had written some basic instructions in fading blue marker.

Step 1. Place a small piece of tape on your forehead.

Step 2. Remove the tape and place it sticky side down on a slide.

Step 3. Use the microscope to look at the slide.

Step 4: Draw what you see.

"Ew, no way am I doing this!" Helsie exclaimed in her twangy accent, tossing her bright blond curls over her shoulder. Liliana glanced over at the table next to theirs where Helsie and her lab partner Katie argued over whose face mites to use. Katie pushed a strand of her short, lavender hair behind her ear and made a throaty scoffing sound.

"Well *I'm* not doing it!" Katie argued back, sliding the tape dispenser toward Helsie. "Do you know how long it took me to do my makeup this morning? I'm not messing up my contouring for this."

Helsie, who wore just as much makeup as Katie did, rolled her eyes.

"Ladies, never fear, Finn is here!" Helsie's boyfriend slid between the girls and ripped off a short piece of tape, slapped it onto his own forehead, then peeled it off. He offered it to Helsie.

"Here you go, babe, you can use my face mites." He leaned over and gave her a kiss on her cheek. She looked at the offered piece of tape stuck to Finn's finger and made a face.

"Somehow that's worse," she whined as her glossy pink lips pursed into a pout.

Finn shrugged and dropped the piece of tape into a nearby trash can. "Your loss. I bet my face mites are super sexy."

Liliana made a point not to look at him, hoping he would wander back to his own table without engaging with her. She really didn't want to talk about the whole crow situation from earlier that morning. Instead of passing by, though, Finn stopped at her table and hopped onto an empty stool. He grinned at Liliana; he was missing one of his top teeth. That, paired with this orange hair, gave him a real jack-o'-lantern look.

"Hey, crow-girl."

"Ha, ha." Liliana rolled her eyes at him. She glanced at Killian and was surprised to see how much smaller he suddenly looked. He seemed to collapse into himself and turned his head down, staring at the microscope in front of him. He fiddled with the knobs uselessly, his pale skin growing pink. Liliana glanced at Finn, then back to Killian. If Killian was trying to make himself invisible, he had failed. Finn had already turned his attention to him, a dangerous spark in his eyes.

"You guys shouldn't have any problem finding face mites," Finn said as he gestured at Killian's acne-crowded face. "Jillian's face must be crawling with them!"

Killian's face grew redder and his hands gripped the microscope tightly. He didn't look up, just stared at the microscope like he was trying to make it explode with his mind.

"Shut up, Finn," Liliana scolded. "And his name is *Killian*, you know that. Don't be a jerk."

Finn threw his hands up as if shielding himself from her words. "Just trying to help!" He grinned again and slapped Killian on the back as he walked past to his own table and waiting science partner.

Liliana turned back to Killian who looked at her like he was trying to make *her* explode with this mind.

"You feel good about yourself?" he spat at her. Liliana leaned back, stunned at his heated tone.

"*What?*"

"You think your half-ass defense makes you a good

person? You're just like him, just like her—" he gestured at Helsie behind her. "You don't get to spend the rest of the day patting yourself on the back for being such a hero. For standing up for your 'loser' lab partner, who you've barely talked to all year."

Liliana's mouth slid open but no words came out. She had no idea what to say. She hadn't been trying to be a *hero;* she just couldn't sit there and not say anything while Finn tortured Killian. Now, though, she wished she'd kept her mouth shut.

She glared back at Killian, trying to control the mixture of hurt and anger swirling around inside of her. She might not have been best friends with him but she'd always been nice to him ... hadn't she? She certainly didn't deserve being snapped at like that.

Killian's stool scraped loudly against the floor as he pushed back from the table. He grabbed his backpack and stormed across the room to the door. Bright sunlight filled the room for a moment, then was snuffed out as the door shut behind him. She hadn't responded to his outburst, just sat there staring at him in silence. She probably made him even more uncomfortable than Finn had.

"Freeeeaaaak," Finn whispered at Liliana from his table. For the briefest of moments she thought he was referring to *her.*

She spent the rest of the period trying to find her own face mites in the microscope and drawing rough photos of the little wormlike creatures she thought she could see in the slide. She drew them with large cartoon eyes and goofy smiles. Making them look cute in her drawing made her feel less grossed out that they were squirming around all over her face.

"Where did Killian go?" Mr. Henderson asked from behind her, making her flinch. Liliana hesitated before answering. She wasn't sure when Mr. Henderson noticed Killian missing and wondered if she cared enough to lie for him. Considering her options, she exhaled and rolled her eyes. She didn't owe him this, and was pretty certain he hated her. But still.

"He had to go to the bathroom," she lied easily. As far as she knew, he *did* have to go to the bathroom.

"Why didn't he ask me first?"

"Ah, it was an emergency. He literally *ran* out, I think—"

"*Oh-kay*, that's enough, thank you Liliana." Mr. Henderson waved away the words she was about to say in disgust. She was disappointed, she'd been ready to really sell it. And if it ended up embarrassing Killian later ... oh well.

The bell rang and she dropped her face mite drawings in the growing pile of papers on Mr. Henderson's desk. Killian hadn't returned, but he wasn't her problem.

Outside the classroom, she snuck another sopapilla out of the hidden container and allowed herself a moment of joy as the sweetness hit her tongue. She eyed the black willow as she chewed, daring the mysterious amber eyes to reappear, but all she saw in the shadows was a lone mourning cloak butterfly, dipping lazily in and out of sight.

5

One boring art class later it was finally lunch time. Liliana entered the cafeteria, a large, echoey room with windows too high for anyone to see out of and buzzing fluorescent lights. Metal picnic tables filled the large open space in tidy rows and overflowing trash cans sat on either side of the room. On the left side was the incredibly inefficient lunch window, the line already painfully long. Liliana joined the other students and waited, annoyed, for her turn to buy lunch. A grouchy woman with brittle, bleach-blonde hair and gray roots scowled at her from the window.

"What do you want?" The woman's voice was gruff and impatient, as if *she* had been the one forced to wait in the long line. Liliana ordered and the woman handed her an overpriced personal-sized pizza in a little cardboard box. She shook it vigorously as she made her way over to her usual table. She enjoyed the sound, the feel, of the pizza ricocheting back and forth against the lid and bottom of the box. It was an old trick; one she'd been doing since junior high. When she opened the box much of the extra grease would be stuck to the inside of the lid instead of pooled on the pizza. Some people used napkins to soak up the puddles of grease, but she found her method much more satisfying.

She approached her group's lunch table and saw that only Ruby and Diego were there. Ruby's waist-long, burgundy hair flowed down her chest and back in wild waves and her hazel eyes were outlined in shimmery blue eye shadow. Her favorite necklace—a long string of shiny red garnets on a gold chain—dripped down her chest and was lost in the cleavage her low cut white tank top revealed. Gold hoop earrings hung from her earlobes and when she smiled, her silver lip ring pressed into her full bottom lip. Diego, Ruby's boyfriend and Liliana's cousin, wrapped one muscled, tan arm around her shoulders but Ruby brushed it away like she always did. Diego was drowning in one of his many too-big T-shirts; Liliana liked to joke he was trying to grow into them. When he wasn't with Ruby, he was usually at the gym lifting.

Liliana glanced around the cafeteria and saw Jeremy a few tables away with his friends. He'd won senior class president by a landslide, and usually hung out with the other guys on the student council. Liliana found it all a bit boring and silly, but he took it seriously, so she tried to as well. They rarely ate lunch together at school, but she'd thought that maybe because today was her birthday ... she let the thought die. It didn't matter, she would spend tonight with him.

She sat on the opposite side of the table from Ruby and Diego and set her pizza box in front of her.

"Happy birthday!" Ruby squealed as she slid a black folder toward her. Ruby had drawn little illustrations in metallic silver pen all over the folder. Liliana turned it every which way to see all the drawings. There was a star constellation, a ram with curled horns, a planet with wide rings around it, poppies, thistles, and some symbols she didn't recognize.

"Ruby, this is beautiful!" Liliana opened the folder to find a stack of papers tucked inside, some full of heavy text, others covered with symbols and moon phases. She glanced back up at Ruby. "What is all this?"

"It's your birthday present! I drew up your birthday for you—your star chart is in there, and your ruling numbers and planets. You are an Aries, the first sign of the zodiac!"

Liliana flipped through the various pages in the folder, uncertain what she was looking at or how she should respond. Ruby was known for becoming obsessed with something and then moving on to the next thing just as quickly. Lately she'd gotten into the zodiac. Liliana gave it about two more weeks before Ruby was onto something else.

"Aries represents the beginning of all things and is ruled by—"

"*¿Qué es?*" Ava interrupted as she dropped her backpack on the bench next to Liliana.

She leaned over Liliana's shoulder to peek at the folder of papers in front of her. She made a breathy noise and rolled her eyes.

"You know some old white dude just made all this up, right? None of this means anything."

Ava sat down on the bench next to Liliana and pulled out a plastic container similar to the one she'd given her that morning. Instead of pillowy fried dough drizzled in honey, this container was filled with Ava's hodgepodge vegetarian lunch. It was usually some combination of protein, vegetables, and carbs. Today it looked like some sort of corn salad with black beans and bell peppers.

Ruby rolled her eyes at Ava and her food, then continued as if she had never been interrupted.

"It's all written out there." Ruby gestured at one of the pages in the folder. "Aries is ruled by Mars, and your element is fire."

Liliana looked down at the folder full of carefully researched birthday information. She felt guilty about how much work Ruby had put into her present, especially because she probably wouldn't read any of it.

Ruby's attention shifted from the folder in front of Liliana to something behind her.

"Gross."

Liliana turned to look at what Ruby was so disgusted by and saw Isabel and her boyfriend Ben making out two tables over. Isabel was sitting in his lap with her arms wrapped around his neck, her fingers in his shoulder-length dusty-brown hair. They looked like they were trying to suck each other's faces off. It was a common, even expected, display at this point. They'd been going out all year and couldn't keep their hands off each other the entire time. Liliana turned back around to face Ruby and shrugged.

"Just don't look."

Ruby scowled and glanced around the cafeteria. "You'd think a teacher would put a stop to it, but noooo, look at them!" Ruby pointed to a couple teachers in the corner standing around talking. Liliana was certain it'd take a lot more than some kissing to interrupt their conversation. The teachers seemed to be as over school as they were.

"God, you're such a prude, Ruby," Ava said as she shoveled a spoonful of corn and bean salad into her mouth.

"I am not!" Ruby grabbed Diego by the arm. "Tell her, Diego."

"Er—" Diego looked, panicked, between Ruby and Ava. "Nah, nah." He shook his head. "I'm not falling for that. There's no right answer here, *¿verdad?*" He glanced at Liliana for help. Liliana smiled and shrugged. *You're on your own.*

Diego was Ruby's boyfriend, but he was also Liliana's cousin, and that meant she *had* to mess with him if given the opportunity. It was practically in the family manual.

Liliana didn't love it when he started dating Ruby but over the last year she'd gotten used to it. Ruby's disgust for public affection made hanging out with them like hanging out with anyone else. They were a couple, but they didn't make a big deal about it.

As she sat there listening to her friends, she felt a soft stab in her chest. She was going to miss them so much. Liliana hadn't told any of them yet, not even Jeremy, that she had gotten into her East Coast dream school and would be leaving at the end of the summer. She wanted to keep things the way they were for as long as possible. She would come back and visit, but she knew it wasn't going to be the same once she left.

Pulling apart her pepperoni pizza, she stuffed a slice, now barely warm, into her mouth. She struggled to swallow the dry bread and cheese as her throat became sore and tight. It hadn't been bothering her for the last hour or so but the pain was back.

It started as a soft buzzing. So quiet, so distant, that she barely noticed it. A hum underneath the chaotic sounds of the cafeteria. She glanced around the room, suddenly overly aware of how loud it was. All around her were voices mixing together, clattering plastic trays, the incessant buzz of the fluorescent lights. She squinted up at the bright sweat-stain-yellow lighting above her and nodded to herself. *It's just the lights*, she thought, relaxing a little.

Liliana turned her attention back to her friends and tried to focus on what Diego was saying. She saw his mouth moving, the humor in his eyes, but she couldn't seem to make out any words. She leaned forward, straining to hear him over the cacophony of cafeteria sounds.

Just as she was about to yell at Diego to speak up, the room went silent.

She could see her friends' mouths moving, people shoving trash into already full trashcans, the cafeteria doors open then slam shut—but she heard nothing. She felt like she'd been plunged under water, suspended in a deep, swallowing silence. Liliana opened her mouth to speak, but before she could get any words out the silence was broken by a soft *snap, crack*.

She tensed as the crackling sound of fire surrounded her. Eyes wide, she scanned the room again, but there were no flames, no heat. The soft crunch of gravel beneath boots made her twist around in her seat, desperately searching for the source of the sound.

Crunch ... crunch ... crunch.

Her heart pounded painfully in her chest, and she tried not to cry as the phantom footsteps came closer ... and closer ...

She was about to scream when the footsteps and the fire transformed into softly whispered words. A chill rippled through her as she felt a cool breath against her ear.

One day, nine hours.

A car horn blared, then the high-pitched scream of wheels sliding across a wet road filled her ears.

Ten years, six months, nine days, this voice whispered.

"Please," she begged no one—everyone. "Please stop."

The sounds didn't stop. They grew louder and more diverse—coming at her from every direction. Glass shattering, waves hitting the shore, a steady mechanical beeping—it was like someone turned the volume on the TV all the way up and was flipping manically through all the channels.

Liliana clutched the table as if she might be thrown off the bench. Voices swirled around her whispering years, days, months. They blurred together.

Eight years, five months, two days. Fifteen years, two months, four days. One year, three months, two days. Eight hours.

Eight hours.

The last voice sounded like sandals slapping sidewalk and a low electrical buzz. As quickly as the voices began,

they stopped. Liliana stared, wide-eyed, at nothing—
her jaw clenched and her hands still gripping the side of
the table.

"Lil, you alright?" Diego asked. "*¿Se siente mal?*" His
thick black eyebrows raised in concern. Ruby and Ava
stopped whatever they were bickering about to look
over at her.

Liliana's mouth fell open but no sound came out.
Her throat was so sore she wasn't sure she'd be able to
talk.

"You didn't hear that?" she asked softly, even though
she already knew the answer. The voices weren't for
them.

They were for *her*.

6

The end-of-lunch bell rang, and Liliana was relieved to escape her friends' concerned expressions and go to her next class. Her hands were trembling at her sides as the last voice echoed inside her mind. The sandals slapping the sidewalk and a low electrical buzzing. They were familiar sounds, commonplace, and yet they made her feel anxious—*walking-alone-at-night* anxious. She glanced furtively behind her, but there was no shadowy figure following her. No danger.

Eight hours.

The other voices she'd been able to understand had been longer periods of time—years, months, days. Something about the shortness of the time frame made her even more nervous. The different time spans made no sense and seemed unrelated to each other, but that last whisper weighed on her.

She floated through the rest of her classes in a fog. The voices that had accosted her in the cafeteria hadn't stayed there—they followed her to her classes, to her locker. They came and went, and every time they quieted, she relaxed a little, only to tense again when they returned.

Liliana wanted to go home, to be done with this day, but instead she forced herself to the girls' locker room for track practice. She had considered skipping it, but ever since lunch her body had been tight with fear, her muscles screaming at her to run. She *needed* to run.

When she got to the locker room, Jeremy was waiting for her outside. He was leaning against the wall, tapping something into his phone, a small smile on his face. He looked up as she approached and stuffed his phone into his pocket.

"Hey," he said with a flirty smile as he pulled her into his arms.

"Hey." She let herself become engulfed in his embrace, buried her head into his chest and tried to keep it together.

"Whoa, what's up?" he pulled away from her slightly and she begrudgingly released her tight grip around him. She wanted to tell Jeremy what was happening to her, to let it all flow out of her in one big loud rush. But as she looked up at him, she couldn't. He wouldn't understand—or even believe—her.

"We still on for dinner tonight?" Jeremy asked.

Liliana closed her eyes and grimaced. She had completely forgotten about her birthday dinner. She had been looking forward to this for the last month—getting dressed up and going out to the restaurant she had chosen. She'd looked at the menu days ago online and already knew what she was going to order. Liliana wasn't going to let a few auditory hallucinations ruin it.

"Of course!" she replied with the best smile she could muster.

"Great, I'll pick you up at six thirty." Jeremy leaned down and gave her a deep kiss that lingered on her lips after he pulled away. "Have fun at practice."

She nodded and was about to say something else, but he'd already started walking away. She shrugged it off and pushed through the locker room doors.

Inside the locker room, voices from the other girls on her team swirled around her, intermixing with a new onslaught of ghostly whispers. She rubbed at her head, willing the voices to stop. She glanced around but didn't see Ava. They'd been doing track together since freshman year, but Ava never made it to practice on time.

Liliana went straight to her locker and changed into her track clothes. She was sitting on a bench lacing up her running shoes when she felt a shadow fall over her. A nauseating baby-powder rose perfume surrounded her like a fog and she felt like gagging. *Becca.*

She looked up warily at the tall, skinny girl looming over her. Becca's dirty-blond hair was pulled into a tight ponytail and her arms were crossed in front of her chest. A cruel smile played on her lips and Liliana braced herself for whatever she was going to throw at her. Becca was the best sprinter on the team and liked to remind everyone of that fact as often as she could. Liliana was a distance runner; they didn't even compete against each other. They got along okay at first, but this year Becca had decided she hated her. Liliana had no idea why. As far as she knew she'd never done anything to Becca.

Becca crinkled her nose as if she smelled something

bad. "Ugh, what is that disgusting smell?" Becca said loudly, drawing the attention of the other girls in the locker room. She didn't need to look to know they were all watching, waiting for whatever Becca's punchline was going to be. Becca leaned down, her thin lips twisted in a nasty smirk Liliana very much wanted to slap right off her face. "Don't you ever shower?"

Liliana stood from the bench but the top of her head barely reached Becca's collarbone. She tilted her head up defiantly, eyes flashing.

"Really, Becca?" a familiar voice said from behind Liliana. She turned to see Ava standing there, her hands on her hips. Her short, dark hair was pushed behind her ears and her black-framed glasses slipped down her nose a little. "You're the one covering up your stink with that awful baby-butt perfume."

Liliana smirked. She didn't need Ava to stand up for her, but it was nice to have a little backup today. Becca glared at Ava, but didn't say anything else before turning and leaving the locker room.

"*¿Por qué es tan perra?*" Ava said as she quickly changed into her own track clothes.

Liliana shrugged and eyed the clock on the wall. "You're late."

"Yeah, yeah, I know." Ava threw her clothes into her locker and slammed the door shut. "I got caught up talking to—someone."

Liliana eyed Ava suspiciously. "*Someone?*"

Ava waved the question away. "I'll tell you later."

Liliana ran laps around the track while Ava practiced the hurdles. Ava didn't have the long legs the other hurdlers on their team had, but she was bouncy. She was able to get up and over as easily as the taller girls. Liliana liked to watch her as she ran, hurdling looked fun but Liliana had fallen flat on her face the one time she'd tried it. She wasn't bouncy like Ava, or fast like Becca, but she had stamina—she could last longer than anyone in a long-distance race. She had the trophies to prove it.

Sweat ran into Liliana's eyes as she ran and she drank the last of the water she had in the bottle she carried with her. She veered off the track and stopped at the water fountain to refill her bottle. Her mother thought she was crazy for being on the track team. The desert heat was intense, but Liliana knew how to manage. Stay hydrated, wear sunscreen, it wasn't complicated.

She ran a few more laps around the track before Coach ended practice. She managed to get into the locker room, grab her stuff, and get out without another irritating interaction with Becca. Liliana waited off to the side for Ava, nodding at some of the other girls on the team as they left the locker room and walked past her.

Liliana fidgeted awkwardly under the weight of her tote bag and started to feel impatient as the locker room continued to empty. She pulled out the container, now only one sopapilla left. She ate it slowly, savoring the last of her birthday treat. She swallowed the last bite just as Ava finally appeared.

Ava nodded at the empty plastic container in Liliana's hand. "Looks like you enjoyed the sopapillas. Or did you end up sharing?"

Liliana thought about how she had snuck the sopapillas, one by one, throughout the day, and felt embarrassed. She should have shared them but they had been the only highlight of an otherwise dark and confusing day. She had felt like she had a right to be selfish, and they were *her* birthday present, after all. Still, she felt a slight flush of shame.

"No, I ate them all," she mumbled as she handed the empty container back to Ava. She took it with a smile and shoved it into her own backpack.

"Good!"

There were hardly any cars left in the parking lot, her own little car sitting alone in a sea of empty white lines. They made their way across the lot, but Ava was distracted, staring at her phone, tapping furiously into it.

"Who are you texting?"

Ava didn't respond as she slid into the passenger seat. Liliana hesitated before getting into the car herself. Ava had been acting weird all day, constantly texting some "no one."

Liliana started the car and pulled out of the school parking lot. Ava's phone buzzed, she read whatever text she had received, then began texting back, her thumbs working the screen relentlessly.

Liliana hit the brakes as a family of quail skittered in front of her car. A *bevy* of quail, she corrected herself silently. She watched them with a mixture of amusement and annoyance. The plump mama quail led six tiny versions of herself across the street without even glancing at Liliana or the heavily exhaling car that almost turned them all into quail pancakes.

Ava didn't even seem to notice, her eyes still glued to her phone.

"Seriously, this is getting annoying," Liliana said as she drove past the quail family and out of the school parking lot. "Who are you texting? Is it the same someone you were caught up talking to before practice? Come on, you're driving me crazy!"

Ava ignored her for a second as she finished texting, then set the phone face down in her lap and looked at her blankly.

"What?"

Liliana rolled her eyes as she slowed to stop at a four-way intersection. "You're really not gonna tell me?"

Ava shrugged. "I'll tell you later."

"Later—*when* later?"

Ava shrugged again and Liliana let out an annoyed huff of breath.

They spent the rest of the ride letting the radio fill the silence, Ava checking her phone frequently while Liliana tried to see who she was texting without crashing her car.

She turned down Ava's street and stopped in front of her house.

"See ya later," Ava said as she grabbed her backpack and jumped out of the car. She hesitated, as if she were going to say something else, but shut the door instead. She gave Liliana a little wave from the other side of the window and then bounded up the driveway to her house.

Liliana watched her go, a prickle of unease crawling

up her spine. Ava was just texting someone. It wasn't a big deal, and yet it set alarm bells off inside of her. She drove the few minutes home deep in thought; the spectral whispers had gone quiet long enough for her to finally *think*. She knew everyone Ava knew, unless Ava had met someone but hadn't told her ... Liliana shook her head, annoyed at herself. She needed to let it go.

As she pulled into her own driveway her eyes fell on the giant walnut tree in their front yard. The branches, full of bright green leaves that morning, were now completely bare and covered in dark, shifting shadows. She put the car in park and stared at the branches of the old tree. A dozen pairs of shining black eyes stared back at her.

The tree was completely full of crows.

"*¡Mierda!*" she hissed under her breath. She'd forgotten about the crows. She was horrified to see that they had never left—but stayed at her house. Waiting for her.

Liliana eyed the short distance from her car to the front door. She would have to pass underneath the tree, underneath the crows, to get inside. She grabbed her tote bag from the car floor and clutched it to her chest like some sort of pathetic armor.

She took a deep breath and slowly eased open the car door, her eyes fixed on the crows. They didn't move as the door opened, didn't move as she slipped out of the car and softly shut the door behind her. They were watching her—every pair of glittering beady eyes following her every movement—but they didn't move.

She bolted toward her house, praying the crows

wouldn't dive-bomb her like they had Ava's dad. Their sharp claws dug into the brittle wood of the walnut tree and their heads shifted slightly to watch her movements, but they stayed in the tree.

Once safely inside, she peered out one of the front windows. She watched the crows, and they watched her back, obsidian eyes gleaming in the fading light. She wondered what her father would say when he came home from work.

Liliana turned from the window and jumped when she saw their three little black Pomeranians sitting a few feet away, poofy little heads turned in her direction. They were all watching her and panting, three little pink tongues lolling from their mouths. They usually jumped all over whoever came into the house, but they had kept their distance from her. She moved slowly around them and their little heads turned to watch her move past, just like the crows.

Liliana rushed to her bedroom, eager to get away from the dogs and the crows and everything else. She passed her brother's room; the door was closed but she could hear him playing a video game and yelling at the screen. She slipped into her own room and shut the door behind her.

Inside her bedroom she relaxed a little. It was quiet in her room, the voices silenced, at least for now. Eying her bed, she struggled against the very strong desire to crawl into it and hide under the covers. She dropped her tote bag onto the bed instead. She needed to know what was happening to her, and there was only one place she could think of to start: the internet.

Liliana sat down at her desk and opened her laptop only to stare dumbly at the screen, not sure what it was she should be searching for. It wasn't like she was doing research for a school paper; this was her life. Her sanity. She wanted answers—but she wasn't sure what to ask.

She typed "hearing voices" into the search engine and didn't like what came up. Psychosis. Bipolar. Schizophrenic. According to the internet, hearing voices usually meant you had some sort of mental illness. But Liliana didn't feel mentally ill, though she guessed no one *feels* mentally ill, they just *are*.

She added "crows" to the "hearing voices" search and hit enter. She frowned at the results as she scrolled through the list. All that came up was information about crows, the sounds they make, and how they can remember human voices. Liliana tapped her fingernails on her desk as she tried to think of the right phrase to search for. She didn't know what else to do, where else to look. She remembered the thought she'd had when she first woke up that morning. That deep, certain feeling that someone was going to die. She typed "knowing someone is going to die, crows" into the search bar.

She didn't love what the results were.

How Crows Know When Someone is Going to Die
Death Omens: Crows
Do Crows Really Sense Death?
Crows and the Paranormal

She clicked on the "Death Omens" result and scrolled through the trashy blog post. Crows were second on the list but none of the other omens meant anything to her.

Black cats, ghostly knocking, an inexplicable chill. She hadn't experienced any of that today, but it didn't really make her feel any better.

She glanced at the time in the top corner of the screen and realized she'd already wasted an hour looking at totally useless search results. She wasn't any closer to knowing what was happening to her and she was still covered in dirt and dried sweat from practice. Slamming her laptop shut, she got up to get ready for her date with Jeremy.

Wrapped in a towel after her shower, she stood in front of her open closet. She had planned on wearing a skin-tight black bodycon dress she'd bought specifically for this date, but now she wasn't so sure. She glanced at the rest of her options—she didn't have a lot of dresses, just a few old prom and homecoming gowns she'd only worn once. Liliana pawed through each dress she owned, hating each one even more than the last. She reached the end of her closet and still hadn't found anything she felt like wearing.

She heard her mother's voice booming from somewhere inside the house, and it was only getting louder. A firm knock on her door made her sigh.

Liliana pulled her towel tighter around her and opened the door an inch to peek out.

"What, Mami?"

Her mother leaned close to the gap in the door, her deep red lips pursed as she took in her undressed daughter.

"Still not dressed yet? When is Jeremy coming to pick you up?"

"Six thirty. I don't know what to wear." Liliana opened the door all the way in defeat, letting her mother into the room.

"Ah, you know, I have an old dress of mine, it doesn't fit me anymore but I bet it will fit you!" Her mother dashed back out of Liliana's room before she could object and disappeared down the hallway toward her own bedroom.

Liliana immediately wished she hadn't told her mother about her wardrobe problem. Whatever she brought back was going to be hideous. She hurriedly looked through her closet again. If she could find something before her mother got back ...

Too late.

Her mother was already back in her room, holding a clover-green dress out to her. It was a simple enough dress, longer than what she usually wore. It was made of a satiny material, not her favorite, but it could have been worse. She scanned her mother's excited, hopeful face and took the dress from her.

"Okay, let me try it on, see if it fits."

Her mother grinned and left the room again, but Liliana could sense her waiting on the other side of the closed door. She dropped her towel on the floor and put her bra and underwear on, then slipped the dress on over her head. She studied her reflection in the full-length mirror hanging on the back of her bedroom door. The dress was longer than she thought it would be, flowing all the way down to her ankles. It was cut low in the back but barely revealed her clavicle in the front. It was more formal than she liked, but Liliana thought it was probably appropriate for the restaurant they were going to. She didn't mind how she looked in it, even sort of liked how romantic and flowy it felt. Plus, it would make her mother happy. She shrugged and opened the door to let her mother see her in it.

Liliana smiled when she saw her mother's face light up. She walked around Liliana, examining how the dress looked on her from every angle.

"*¡Espléndida!*" she exclaimed, clapping her hands happily. "I used to love this dress, but I'm fat now, *te culpo a ti y a tu hermano.* You two stole my body!"

Liliana rolled her eyes and wrapped an arm around her mother's shoulders. "You're not fat, Mamá, you know that."

Her mother pouted and put her hands around her own midsection. "I miss having a waist."

Liliana sighed, she'd heard this whole bit a hundred times before and wasn't in the mood to hear it again now.

"Okay, thanks for the dress, now go, *sal de aquí!*" She shooed her mother out of her bedroom. "I have to finish getting ready before he gets here."

"*¿Tienes zapatos?*" her mother called over her shoulder as Liliana ushered her out.

"*Sí*, I have shoes, thank you!"

She finally got the door shut and let out an annoyed breath. She loved her mother but she could be a lot.

Liliana fished a pair of black heels out of the bottom of her closet and considered the three purses she owned: a brown one, a black clutch, and a cream-colored hobo bag. She grabbed the black clutch since it matched her shoes and shoved her cell phone, wallet, and a tube of burgundy lipstick inside.

She was fixing her hair when she heard her phone buzz from inside the clutch. She took it out and looked at the screen.

Jeremy: *I'm here.*

She texted back *coming* and shoved the phone back into the clutch. Liliana took one last look at herself in the mirror, her dark, wavy hair fell around her like a shroud and the green shift dress made her look like a Grecian princess. She had to admit—she didn't hate it.

Liliana grabbed a light jacket and made her way to the front door as quietly as she could. She was really hoping she could sneak out before her mother or father saw her and made her do something embarrassing like take pictures. When she made it outside without running into anyone she let out a breath of relief. She snapped her eyes up to the walnut tree, but the crows were no longer there. Without the crows, the tree looked strangely lonely—the bare branches brittle and gray. She didn't know anything about trees, but she'd grown up with this one in her front yard. She'd seen it in every season, every state, but she'd never seen it like this before.

It looked *dead*.

7

Jeremy waited in his idling black Jeep on the street in front of her house. She could see him through the car window tapping something into his phone. He put it down when she opened the door and stepped up into the car.

Jeremy smiled at her and eyed the green dress she was wearing.

"What's that shiny material?" he said as he pinched a piece of the skirt between two fingers.

"Uh, I don't know—satin, maybe?" she looked down at the dress and started second-guessing her choice. She briefly considered running back inside to change into the black bodycon dress, but she didn't want to run into her parents. They'd be late for the dinner reservation, anyway.

"Hm," he said, dropping the fabric and putting both hands on the steering wheel. "It's not very flattering."

Liliana looked down at the dress again, her face burning with embarrassment. He was right, it *wasn't* very flattering. Her mood turned sour as she thought about how her mom had practically forced her to wear it. She was annoyed with herself for not picking her own outfit.

Jeremy drove them out of the neighborhood and onto one of the main arterial streets but blew past where she knew the turn was. *Maybe we're just going a different way,* she thought. With each turn he took, the more certain she became that they were not heading toward the restaurant. In fact, it seemed like they were heading to …

"Why are we driving toward your house?" Liliana asked slowly. "I thought we were going to La Papillon?"

"Yeah, about that …" Jeremy looked over at her briefly, flashing her a mischievous grin. Liliana returned his smile with a frown.

"We're not going out to dinner, are we?"

"Nope! But I promise this is going to be so much better, you'll see."

Liliana forced herself to smile back and turned away to look out the window. She could see her reflection in the darkened glass, her heart-shaped face surrounded by dark, wavy hair. Her eyes looked like shadows, dark and empty. She looked disappointed. She *was* disappointed.

Liliana had gotten all dressed up just to go to Jeremy's house. She felt a familiar ache in her chest, in her throat, but not the ache she'd been feeling all day. This was the ache of trying not to cry. *Stop it,* she reprimanded herself. *You're being so stupid right now. It's just dinner.*

She tried to imagine how going to his house for the hundredth time was better than going to the restaurant she'd been wanting to try for months. The *one* thing she had wanted to do. She remembered the small present he'd shown her that morning and immediately felt like a spoiled brat. Whatever he had planned she would try to enjoy. She stared at herself in the window, forcing her face into a happier, less grumpy shape.

Jeremy lived further back into the Catalina Foothills than she did, in a sprawling, light-filled house on an acre of open desert. His house loomed above the city, surrounded by stoic saguaros, flowering barrel cacti, and chunks of rock in sunset colors. Jeremy turned onto the long driveway that led through the property and to the house, the road winding around cactus and small boulders. When they reached the house, it was all lit up from the inside, and Liliana groaned internally at the realization she would have to interact with Jeremy's parents. They were polite to her, but she always had the distinct impression they weren't thrilled with Jeremy's choice of girlfriend.

Jeremy opened the car door for her and she got out, her green dress sticking to the backs of her damp thighs. She peeled the skirt off her legs and followed Jeremy to the front door, a massive oak monstrosity with ornate carvings and actual little iron knockers shaped like roses. She'd always thought those knockers were rather tacky and refused to use them when she went to Jeremy's house. She would knock on the door with her fist instead, and though his parents never said anything she was pretty sure they could hear the difference.

He opened the door and led her inside, the familiar cream walls and matching cream carpet greeted her as it always did. She secretly hated Jeremy's house. Everything a shade of beige, everything delicate and unnecessarily bougie. Blown-glass roses rested inside a blown-glass vase on a small glass entryway table. Knock-off Monet watercolors—at least she *thought* they were knock offs—were scattered around the house. She always felt like she didn't belong there, that given even a moment alone she'd manage to knock furniture over, stain the carpet, break things. She stayed close to Jeremy as she looked around for his parents, but the house was empty.

"My parents are out of town," Jeremy answered the unspoken question. "Won't be back until Sunday." He grinned at her and she relaxed a little, relieved that she'd at least be spared an awkward interaction with his parents.

Liliana sniffed the air—usually Jeremy's house smelled like expensive candles or cleaning supplies, but tonight there was a spice to the air, the scent of something familiar wafting from the kitchen. She looked at Jeremy, confused.

"Is someone else here?"

He grinned again. "You'll see, but not yet! Come on, let's go out onto the patio."

Liliana followed Jeremy obediently, letting him lead her through the house and outside onto the sprawling back patio. Twinkly café lights lit up the area, wrapped around the trellis, and a fire wavered and crackled inside the outdoor beehive fireplace. The long picnic table had a line of lit white candles in the center. It was beautiful. It was also a fire hazard.

"You left all this burning while you picked me up?"

"Surprise!" a new voice called from behind her.

Liliana jumped and turned to see Ruby, her burgundy

hair now curled into messy ringlets, coming at her with open arms. She'd changed out of the clothes she wore earlier into a long dress the color of daffodils. It was a bad color on her, and clashed with her deep red hair, but Liliana certainly wasn't going to say anything about it. She let Ruby wrap her into a lavender-scented hug.

Liliana pulled away, smiling. "I just saw you like three hours ago!"

"I know! But this time it's a *surprise*."

"Uh, huh." Liliana eyed Jeremy and tried to shoot him a *what is going on* message telepathically, but he must have missed it because he disappeared into the house without responding. A second later Diego took his place, two uncapped beers in his hands. He handed one to Ruby and paused, then held the other out to Liliana.

"Oh hey, didn't realize you were already here. You want a beer?"

Liliana shook her head no, then turned back to Ruby. "What is all this? What's going on?"

"It's your birthday party!"

That's what Liliana was afraid of. She eyed the sliding glass door nervously, wondering who else would be showing up. Diego leaned in close to Liliana and gave her a friendly nudge.

"Don't worry, cuz, it's just us and Ava."

Ava, of course. The enticing smells from the kitchen had to be her doing.

Liliana looked up at the long stretch of darkening sky above her. She could just make out a few early stars, a thin crescent ghost of a moon.

Ava and Jeremy appeared, carrying a heavy cast-iron pan between them. They placed it in the center of the table with a thud that rattled the wine glasses at each setting. With a flourish Ava removed the lid of the pan to reveal the most gorgeous paella Liliana had ever seen. Saffron-stained rice with chunks of red sausage, mussels still in their obsidian shells, and fat shrimp with their heads still on.

"Ava, no! This is amazing!" Liliana cried out, pulling out her phone to take photos of the culinary masterpiece.

"That's not all," Ava said as she pulled a bottle of red wine from her bag. "I stole this from my stepmom's wine rack." Ava examined the label, then shrugged. "I'm pretty sure she just buys wine based on how much she likes the label. This could be ten dollars or a hundred dollars as far as I know."

Ava unscrewed the top and poured bright, cranberry-red wine into their glasses, then sat next to Liliana. Ava held up her phone and Liliana squinted at the text chain she was showing her. It was a series of back-and-forths between her and ...*Jeremy*. She gave Ava a questioning look.

"Who I've been texting all day, had to help him plan all this," she explained as she gestured at the dining table.

Liliana looked at everything from the gorgeous paella Ava made to the wine Ava brought and wondered what exactly *Jeremy* had contributed. She glanced up at the pretty tealights twinkling above them.

Liliana tried to drink the wine and enjoy the paella,

but it was hard. The voices came and went, like an ocean tide. The whispers all said different things, all sounded different. Like before, she was able to make words out of what should be just sounds.

Fifty-two years, one month, eight days. A mechanical beeping.

Sixty-five years, three months, twelve days. A soft exhale of breath.

One day, two hours. Fire crackling, dirt crunching underneath boots. All of the voices were vaguely familiar, but the short time frame of the last one bothered her. *Is something going to happen tomorrow? Something bad?*

"Okay, birthday girl, you're first," Ruby said with a grin.

Liliana looked up, confused. The table had been cleared, and Ruby was sitting across from her holding a deck of oddly large playing cards. Liliana scanned the rest of the group; they were all drinking beer or wine and appeared relaxed. They didn't seem to know Liliana had been zoning out. She had no idea how much time had passed, no memory of her plate being taken away. The glass of wine in front of her was half full. She wasn't sure if she had finished a glass and it'd been refilled or if she had barely touched it.

Across from her, Ruby separated a small group of cards from the deck and put the rest of them aside. "I just got these, I only know how to do one spread, and I only know the Major Arcana cards—they're the fun ones, anyway." Ruby shrugged, her hoop earrings shivering from her earlobes.

Liliana caught Jeremy's eye and he smirked. *This ought to be good,* the look said. She looked closer at the cards in Ruby's hands and recognized them, vaguely, as tarot cards. *Oh, God, she's going to do a tarot reading,* Liliana groaned internally. *This is the last thing I need right now.*

Ruby fanned out the cards in her hands and offered them to Liliana. "Okay, pick three cards and without looking at them place them in a row face down in front of you."

Liliana tried not to roll her eyes as she pulled three cards at random from the fan and did as she was told. Ruby pushed the remaining cards together into a small deck and set them aside.

"Okay, so these three cards represent your past, present, and future," Ruby explained as she tapped each card with one long crimson-painted nail. "Go ahead and flip over the one on the far left."

Liliana didn't believe in this stuff, yet she could feel her heart beating a little faster. She took a deep breath to try and loosen the tightness in her chest. *You're being stupid,* she chastised herself. She flipped the first card over. A beautiful woman with calm, sea-blue eyes stared up at her. *The Empress* was scrawled in cursive at the bottom of the card.

Ruby leaned over to get a better look, then consulted a little booklet she held in her hand.

"You know you're really taking the magic out of this," Diego teased, "reading from a booklet."

"Shut up, I'm still learning," Ruby snapped, then turned back to the booklet. "Okay, so the left card speaks to things in the past that are still affecting you. The Empress represents family, security, and love. Aw, that's nice."

Liliana smiled thinking about her mother, the eighteen kisses she plastered all over her face that morning. Her father handing her the thermometer. Her brother scowling at her over his book.

"Okay, flip over the middle card now, this represents your present."

Liliana hesitated. Her present had been rather chaotic and dark lately, and she was worried what she would see staring up at her. She shook away the thoughts again, willing herself to not be such a baby.

She flipped the second card over and a lightning-struck tower appeared. Liliana relaxed; a tower didn't seem so bad.

"Oh, no," Ruby said in a small voice as she looked from the card to the booklet and back again.

"What?"

"Well, ah, The Tower is ... well sort of the worst card you could get."

"Ruby!" Diego hissed, nudging her. "It's her birthday!"

"Hey, man, I didn't pick the card, she did!"

"You could have just lied, none of this means anything anyway."

Ruby glared at Diego and he grinned back at her, then puckered his lips for a kiss. Ruby rolled her eyes but Liliana saw the hint of a smile as she turned away from Diego.

"What does it mean? The Tower?" Liliana asked, her

mouth felt dry, her throat swollen and sore again.

"It means ... it means bad things are coming."

Someone is going to die.

The thought echoed inside of her as it had since she opened her eyes that morning. *It's just a stupid card game,* she told herself firmly.

"I'm kind of scared to flip over the last one," she admitted.

"You don't have to," Ruby said and raised her hand over the cards. Liliana grabbed her wrist before she could sweep them back into the deck.

"No, it's fine, I want to see."

Liliana didn't hesitate this time but reached down and flipped the card over a little harder than she meant to.

She should have known what card it would be. A figure in a long, gray cloak with a scythe in its hand.

Death.

"This actually isn't a bad card!" Ruby insisted, a little too loudly. Liliana snorted; she couldn't help herself. How could *Death* not be a bad card?

"No, really, look!" Ruby offered Liliana the small booklet she'd been reading from. Liliana took it begrudgingly and read the short blurb under Death. *Change is coming. The end of one thing, the beginning of another.*

That didn't really make Liliana feel any better. She handed the booklet back to Ruby.

"So, what's next, Ruby, you want to do a séance? A fun little birthday ghost-chat?" Jeremy chided as he wrapped an arm around Liliana. She stared down at the three cards, lying face up on the table in front of her. *Empress, Tower, Death*. She examined the Death card and felt unsettled as she stared into the darkness inside the gray hood where a face should be. Ruby's ring-adorned hand broke her focus as she swept the three cards out of sight and back into the deck.

"Anyone else want a turn?" Ruby asked the group, her tone wavering as she clumsily shuffled the deck.

"Hard pass." Ava said as she finished off her glass of wine.

A cold breeze blew across Liliana's skin and she shivered underneath Jeremy's arm. Her sore throat was getting worse and she could feel her pulse in her windpipe. She shifted uncomfortably under Jeremy's arm and tried to swallow, but couldn't. It felt like her throat was full of hardening concrete. A hot surge of panic rushed through Liliana, her heart beating faster and faster, thundering in her chest so hard it hurt. She gasped, her hands flying to her throat, her nails scratching at her skin. *I can't breathe*, she realized. *I can't breathe!*

She stared, wild-eyed, at her friends as they watched her, their faces all pinched in confusion. As she got lightheaded and the twinkly cafe lights dimmed, an overwhelming urge to scream filled her. She opened her mouth and let out a shriek she didn't hear as everything went black.

8

Liliana bit into her thumbnail and cringed internally as she felt a piece of the nail tear off. She spat the nail remnant out onto the street and sucked at the tiny droplets of blood oozing from her ripped cuticle. She was in motion, her body moving forward down the street past tidy cream, beige, and sage-green houses. Except it wasn't her body. She was taller, thinner, weaker. She wanted to look down at herself but had no control over the body she was inside.

It was colder than it had been at Jeremy's house. Darker. The lights in most of the houses were off, darkened windows stared at her from either side.

She was walking faster now. Liliana had no control of her legs but she could feel the increase in speed. She looked over her shoulder once, twice.

Liliana felt the girl's terror as if it were racing through her own body. Adrenaline drowned her mind—or the girl's mind—Liliana wasn't sure anymore where she ended and the other girl began.

I'm scared of something, Liliana thought, trying to calm herself with deduction. *Something is following me. Her.*

When she started running, Liliana *knew* this wasn't her body. She knew exactly how every muscle, every ligament, felt when she ran, and this was all wrong. Liliana already had a pinch in her side, and her calves felt like they were on fire. This body was not a runner's body. She focused on her feet for the first time, hearing the *slap slap slap* of her sandals as she ran, the bite of the rubber straps between her toes.

Flip flops. I can't believe I'm running in flip flops.

One of the shoes caught on the ground and the cheap material folded over, underneath her foot. Her body tipped forward and she fell down onto the pavement, catching herself with her hands. Pain exploded in her palms, her wrists, her knees. The girl's straight, silky hair slid across her face and tears welled up in her eyes as she stared down at the concrete sidewalk. She was breathing hard, a rattling, aching sound filled with terror. A long shadow fell over her, cutting off the dim glow of the buzzing nearby streetlight.

Her body tensed, her limbs frozen and stiff. She heard a low hissing sound emanating from the shadow looming over her, but she couldn't move. Couldn't look behind her. Liliana was filled with this odd feeling—if she didn't look, didn't *see* it, then it didn't exist. A hot, sharp pain exploded in the center of her back; her veins felt like they were on fire as an excruciating burning ripped through her body. She tried to call out, to scream, to beg—but the only sound she made was a soft whimper as her body slumped to the ground.

9

When Liliana opened her eyes she was staring up at the night sky—flicks of stars decorating the world's ceiling. She wasn't in the street, but on Jeremy's deck, her head resting in his lap. Warm tears squeezed out of the corners of her eyes and trickled down her temples. Jeremy leaned over her, blocking out the sky—and everything else—behind him. Diego was squatting nearby, looking down at her with concern. Ava stood next to him, a plastic baggy of ice in her hands; the twinkling tea lights reflected in her glasses.

She remembered everything. Running, falling, dying. She felt different than she had before, like some tiny piece of her had been hollowed out.

"What happened?" she murmured as she sat up slowly with Jeremy's help. "How long was I out for?"

"A few minutes," Ava said, offering her the bag of ice. Liliana stared at it, not sure what she was supposed to do with it.

"*No sé,*" Ava answered Liliana's confused expression with a shrug. "It seemed like the thing you do?"

"Ice?" Ruby scoffed as she came out of the house and walked toward them, a steaming mug in her hands.

"No, she needs heat."

Ruby handed Liliana the mug and Liliana stared at it—it had a photo printed on it of Jeremy's parents when they were young, grinning out at her from a wind-whipped sailing boat. A string hung out of the steaming water with a small tag attached.

"It's chamomile tea," Ruby told her, though she hadn't asked. She didn't care, tea couldn't fix this. She set the mug down on the ground next to the baggy of ice.

"Are you okay? You looked like you were choking and then you screamed and fainted," Diego said crouching in front of her, his eyes searching hers for some sort of clue. "Should we take you to the hospital ... or ... ?"

"No! No, that's not—I don't need—" Liliana didn't know what to tell him, to tell any of them. There was nothing a hospital could do—no pill or cough drop or shot was going to fix this. Something was *very* wrong. Something she could no longer ignore or pretend away.

As Jeremy rubbed gentle circles on her back she could feel the ghost of the searing pain she'd felt moments earlier, in that other body. She cringed, wishing he would stop touching her.

She looked at her friends, all four of them staring back at her with matching worried expressions. A wine bottle nearby was still half full and she reached over and grabbed it by the neck. She tipped it up and took a deep drink, then set the bottle back down with a soft thud and wiped a dribble of wine from her chin. Her throat, which had been hot and swollen before, now felt fine.

She picked up her phone and looked at the time. It

was only 8:32 p.m. but exhaustion weighed down her body and no part of her wanted to keep partying, not after what she had just gone through. She wanted to go home. She wanted to forget everything that she'd just experienced. She wanted her birthday to be *over*.

Liliana turned to Jeremy and gave him a weak smile.

"Sorry, I'm not feeling so great. Could you take me home?"

Jeremy frowned. "Are you sure? Maybe you just need a few minutes and then—"

"No, sorry, thank you, all of you, for this," Liliana said, gesturing at the twinkling tea lights, the wine, and what was left of the giant pan of paella. She stood and grabbed her jacket and purse, slipping her phone inside. "I'm just really tired, I need to go to bed."

Jeremy looked as if he wanted to argue, but didn't. Instead, he nodded and grabbed his car keys.

Liliana drowned in the uncomfortable silence as Jeremy drove her back to her house. She could sense that he was mad at her, but she couldn't deal with that right now. She didn't feel like she could deal with *anything* right now. All she wanted to do was to crawl into bed and hide under the covers. Maybe she would wake up tomorrow and all of this would have just been one dark day of her life and everything would go back to normal.

"So are you going to tell me what's going on, or..." Jeremy asked after a few minutes. He didn't look at her, his eyes pinned to the road.

Liliana considered it, she really did. She wanted desperately to talk about what had been happening to her all day, what had *just* happened to her. But Jeremy wasn't the one to talk to. He'd try to explain it all away the same way she tried to, and she was past that now. She was done denying the truth, even if she wasn't quite sure what that truth was.

"Nothing is going on," she replied softly as she turned away to stare out her window. She didn't want him to see the lies in her eyes. "I'm just tired."

Jeremy let out a disappointed breath and didn't ask again.

When he stopped the car outside of her house, she could see her mother sitting on the front porch. Swirls of smoke were coming off of her cigarette and Liliana shook her head unhappily. She got out of the jeep but lingered with the door open. She didn't know what she wanted to say. She had ruined everything, but it wasn't really her fault. There was no way for her to explain that to him—not in a way he would understand.

"Jeremy, I—"

"Here." He held out the small silver-wrapped present he'd shown her that morning. She'd forgotten all about it. That morning felt like a year ago, now. The guilt inside her swished back and forth. She'd ruined the party he'd planned for her, forgotten about the gift entirely. *I am the worst.*

She hesitated but took the present. She wondered if he wanted her to open it now, in front of him, after everything.

"Open it later." Jeremy's hands were back on the steering wheel, and he was looking straight ahead, his jaw tight. She stood there, shivering in the cold, holding the little present, and wondered how things had gone so wrong.

"I'm sorry, I've just been feeling really off today, and I just need to go to sleep. We're okay, right?"

There was a long, painful moment of silence.

"Happy birthday," he finally said, a tinge of sarcasm in his voice that made Liliana feel like she'd been punched in the chest. Then, "Shut the door."

Liliana's face tingled as the blood rushed out of it. He was *really* angry. She paused, wanting to say more but not knowing what to say, so she said nothing. She shut the door and watched as the truck sped off and disappeared around the corner. A painful ache filled her chest and she had the urge to throw up. She felt the tears coming, but forced them back. She didn't want her mother to see her crying.

Liliana walked up her driveway, the little silver-wrapped present in her hand. She slipped it into her purse as she walked up the steps to the porch. Her mother was sitting on one of the old rocking chairs they kept out there, a black clove cigarette in her right hand, the spicy smell of the cloves and vanilla scenting the air around her. She wore a thick, dark-pink bathrobe over her pajama pants and oversize shirt she usually slept in. Her dark, gray-streaked hair pulled on top of her head in a messy bun.

"Clove cigarettes are just as bad for you as regular cigarettes, you know." Liliana sat down in the empty chair next to her. "Worse, even."

Her mother brought the cigarette to her lips and Liliana heard the familiar crackle as her mother inhaled. She exhaled a plume of gray smoke into the night air and put the cigarette out in the poorly formed clay ashtray she had made, a companion to the hideous key dish inside the house.

"I know, but it's not every day *mi niña pequeña* turns eighteen, I'm celebrating and mourning at the same time. All grown up."

Liliana didn't feel all grown up. After the events of the day, of the night, all she wanted was her mother to wrap her in one of her suffocating hugs.

"Were you waiting for me out here?" Liliana asked as she rocked gently in the chair.

"*Sí y no,*" her mother replied.

Liliana didn't look at her but watched the street in front of her house instead. She hoped if she didn't meet her mother's eyes she wouldn't know how upset she was. The last thing she wanted to talk about was Jeremy.

They both turned when they heard the familiar *tap, tap, tap* of hooves as a small herd of javelinas trotted down the street. Their piggish noses led them to trash cans, gardens, anything remotely edible. Most people in the neighborhood thought they were a nuisance, a danger to their pets and destroyer of their vegetable gardens, but Liliana secretly loved them. They were so cute. She never saw them during the day, but at dusk and nighttime they would appear as if from thin air.

Liliana and her mother sat in silence as they watched the javelinas, the boarish animals giving them the occasional disinterested glance as they trotted past their house.

"You're home earlier than I thought you'd be."

Liliana's mother rarely asked straightforward

questions; she preferred to make "openings" as she liked to call them. Statements that offered the other person a chance to share something, if they wanted to, but vague enough to be ignored if they *didn't* want to. It was something Liliana always appreciated about her mother.

She considered what her response should be. She could not respond at all, just sit quietly in the cold, rocking. But what had happened to her was fresh in her mind, in her body, and she didn't think another internet search was going to answer any of her questions.

"Mamá, something ... I think something is happening. To me." She felt stupid uttering the words, she hadn't thought this through. She hadn't decided what to tell her mother and what to leave out. What was important, what wasn't?

Her mother nodded, a faraway look in her eyes.

"You know, when I was about your age, all the roses in your abuela's garden died."

Liliana blinked, a touch of intrigue rippled through her. "What?"

"The walnut tree." Her mother gestured with a hand smeared with dried black paint. "It's dead."

Liliana looked at the old tree. She'd collected the walnuts from it, the soft brown morsels hidden inside leaf-green balls, every fall for as long as she could remember. The tree should be starting to bud by now, leaves unfurling, but instead the branches were bare and ashen.

"You know, it's funny, your grandmother didn't seem surprised when the roses died. It was almost as if she expected it to happen. She loved those roses, she'd won contests with them, before they all died, of course. She just dug up the dead plants and threw them away. Didn't even bother planting new ones."

"Why is that funny?" Liliana was watching her mother now, but her mother was watching some memory-movie inside her head, her eyes wide and glassy.

"It's funny because that walnut tree is probably over one hundred years old. It's one of the reasons I wanted to buy this house." She turned to look at Liliana, reached over, and took her hand. "And now that it's dead, I'm not even surprised."

Liliana felt guilty, but she didn't know why. *She* hadn't killed the tree. Had she?

"We should call someone to remove it," her mother continued, dropping Liliana's hand as she stood from her rocking chair. "It could fall over and crush one of the cars."

Liliana stared at the dead walnut tree, its large branches reached over their driveway, but had been pruned away from the house. Liliana didn't understand how a tree could just die overnight like that. Then again, there were a lot of things she couldn't understand lately.

"Come inside, it's cold out here," her mother said, gesturing for Liliana to follow. "I'll make you your birthday treat."

Liliana had forgotten about the cooked peaches and ice cream. She was full from dinner and her sweets allotment for the day had been more than satisfied by Ava's sopapillas, but she had promised her mother to save room.

She followed her inside the house and found Mateo sitting at the dining table, working on homework.

"Isn't it past your bedtime?" Liliana teased, ruffling his hair as she passed by. He scowled and rolled his eyes but didn't respond. Liliana sat down at the table across from her brother, dropping her clutch onto the table next to her.

Her mother went to the stove and turned it on, placed a pan on top of the burner and poured olive oil into it. She pulled two peaches from the fruit basket on the counter and sliced them into almost even pieces.

"*¿Dónde esta Papá?*" Liliana asked.

"Emergency call," her mother answered. "There was another attack, at a goat farm not too far from here. Coyotes are out of control. They have no fear of humans anymore. Come right down from the hills and snack away on whatever they please. I should call your abuela, warn her. She'd be devastated if something happened to one of her horses."

Her mother dropped the peach slices into the hot pan with a large amount of cinnamon. She watched as they sizzled and flipped them as they began to caramelize. She divided the peaches into two bowls and added a large scoop of vanilla ice cream on top of each. She placed the bowls in front of Liliana and Mateo, then sat down in an empty chair.

Mateo pushed aside his homework and attacked the dessert as if he were starving.

"You're not having any?" Liliana asked her mother.

"No, you two enjoy."

Liliana ate delicately, small bites, trying to ease the

food into her already overly full stomach. She hadn't had the chance to tell her mother about anything that had happened, derailed by the story about her abuela's roses and the dying walnut tree. Now, in the warmth of the kitchen, with her traditional birthday dessert in front of her, it all started to feel like a strange dream she'd woken up from. Lingering, but not real.

Her brother finished first and dumped his dirty bowl and spoon into the sink before slinking off to his bedroom. Her mother usually would have snapped at him to rinse the dish and put it in the dishwasher, "*What am I, your servant?*" But this time she didn't. She had a faraway look, distracted by her own thoughts.

"Well, I'm exhausted," Liliana said, standing and putting her bowl, then Mateo's, into the dishwasher. "Thanks for dessert, Mamá." She leaned down and kissed her mother's smooth cheek.

Her mother looked up at her, almost as if she was surprised to see her standing there. "Oh, of course *mija*. Happy birthday."

Liliana smiled and started down the hallway to her bedroom when the sound of her mother's voice stopped her.

"You know, there's always been something ... different ... about the Presagio women." Liliana turned back around and took a few slow steps back into the kitchen.

"You should ask your abuela, she—" her mother was cut off as the front door banged open. They both turned to see Liliana's father drop his medical bag on the floor and shut the door behind him. Liliana eyed his clothes and wrinkled her nose—they were covered in dirt, hay, and blood. He looked pale and exhausted, a dark sadness in his eyes Liliana was all too familiar with.

His patient—or patients—hadn't survived.

"Jesus, David!" Her mother stood from the table and rushed to her husband. "What happened?"

"Mrs. Willard, up the hill. Her pet goats were attacked. Blood everywhere—their throats torn out—" David glanced at Liliana standing a few feet away. "Ah, sorry honey, you don't want to hear this."

Three little black shadows emerged from underneath the dinner table and began sniffing at her father's blood-soaked pants.

"I better get these off and in the wash."

Her father turned and headed the opposite direction toward her parents' bedroom. Her mother shot her an apologetic look and followed her husband, and the three Pomeranians followed her mother, leaving Liliana alone in the kitchen. The coppery smell of fresh blood lingered in the air; she could practically taste the metallic flavor of it in her mouth.

She fled the kitchen and relaxed only once her bedroom door was shut behind her.

Liliana's mind struggled to organize all the information she'd gathered in the last few hours. How did it all fit together? She dropped her clutch on her desk, then remembered Jeremy's silver-wrapped gift. She pulled the small box out and stared at it in her hand miserably.

This wasn't how she was supposed to feel about a gift from her boyfriend, on her birthday. She should be happy, excited, but all she felt was guilty and a little nauseous.

Liliana didn't want to open it, not like this. She set it on her desk instead, hoping she'd feel differently in the morning. Hoping everything would be back to normal when she woke up tomorrow.

10

Liliana woke up with a sore throat again, itchy and swollen. Last night's events swirled inside her head and she buried her face into her pillow. It all felt like a bad dream, being chased inside someone else's body, her ruined birthday party, her mother's cryptic story about her abuela's roses. She had hoped when she woke up everything would be back to normal and she could pretend none of that happened.

But here she was again, with that same feeling of dread inside of her—that heavy knowledge that someone was going to die. *No,* she insisted, pushing the feeling deep inside of her along with the dark memories of the night before. *It's over. I'm moving on. Everything is going to be fine.*

Liliana got out of bed, determined to go back to her normal life. Her normal routines. She changed into her running clothes and shoes and pulled her long hair into a ponytail. She slipped quietly out of the house, everyone, even her mother, still asleep.

Outside it was barely dawn, the sky still dark, showing fading stars. Shades of periwinkle and lavender bloomed against the backdrop of the Catalina Foothills where the sun would soon inch up and over. She started a slow jog down her usual route, her sneakers slapping pavement until she turned left onto a dirt trail that led up into the base of the foothills. Houses disappeared behind her as she ran, replaced with towering saguaros, fat barrel cacti, and golden-flowered brittlebush.

Liliana relished the cool air blowing against her as she ran. Soon the sun would rise and it would get horribly hot, but now, during the quiet dawn, it was still comfortable. She'd run this trail a hundred times before, her morning routine if there wasn't a morning track practice scheduled. She expertly avoided the spiky cholla cacti that reached out into the trail with their many prickly fingers and easily dodged the peppering of snake holes.

Almost at the top of the first hill, her usual turn-around point, she slid on some loose rocks. She faltered and fell backward, landing hard on her back against the rocky trail. Her right arm burned, and she saw several long scratches starting to ooze blood where a nearby cactus had scraped her. She was more embarrassed than hurt. This was *her* trail; she knew it as well as her own bedroom. She felt a strange sense of betrayal. Liliana pushed herself up off the ground and wiped her dirty hands on her shorts, then froze. An oddly familiar hissing noise, like something she'd heard in a dream once, was coming from somewhere in the desert.

She glanced nervously around the trail looking for snakes, but they were never out this early and the trail was empty. Besides, the only noise to fear was the rattle, not the hissing. There was no rattling, but a crunching sound had started to accompany the hissing—and it was getting closer. In the distance she saw a saguaro shudder then tip forward, landing with a thud onto the ground. Then another saguaro fell, and she squinted into the rising sun, trying to see what was happening to the cacti.

The crunching sound stopped. She turned every which way, looking for whatever animal was causing all the damage, and stopped when she saw the sun hit something smooth and black. The light glinted off the obsidian shell of a scorpion bigger than she was, its dagger tail high in the air.

She took a step backward and blinked rapidly, not understanding what it was she was seeing. It was a scorpion—but the front half of the creature looked ... *human.*

The front of the scorpion's body melted into a man's torso—covered in the same shiny, black shell as the rest of the body. His head was covered in too many eyes and tiny pincers were where his mouth should have been. The man's arms were giant—overly large for the rest of his body, and ended in razor-edged pincers that snapped together menacingly.

Liliana took another slow step backward, her stomach tightening with a strong urge to vomit. Her eyes fell to the monster's scorpion portion and she gagged. Instead of smooth, segmented scorpion legs, muscular human arms jutted out on each side of the scorpion's body, palms pressed against the desert floor. She stared, horrified, at the thick fingers digging into the dirt. It took a step closer to her, the hissing sound deafening.

She should run. Scream. Throw something at the monster—but she couldn't move. Her brain had simply ... broken. She couldn't think clearly, didn't know what to do. All she could do was stand there, stupidly looking at the creature that was going to kill her.

The scorpion burst into movement, scuttling toward her so fast there was no way she would be able to outrun it. In a matter of seconds it had closed the distance between them, and it was so close she could see the droplets of hot poison dripping from the tip of its tail high above her.

She had woken up knowing someone was going to die—she just hadn't realized it was going to be *her*.

A small flash of dark red caught her attention, and she risked ripping her gaze from the monster to see what it was. There, a few yards away in the shadow of a saguaro, was a fox. The fox watched her with sharp amber eyes, its long, bushy tail swishing so swiftly it looked like he had more than one. Liliana recognized those eyes; they were the same ones that had been watching her from behind the black willow tree at school the day before.

The fox opened its mouth, displaying small, sharp white teeth, and let out a high-pitched screech that made her cover her ears. The scorpion monster took a few steps back, its hideous multi-eyed head twisting side to side looking for what made the noise.

Run. Now.

Liliana wasn't sure if she'd heard the voice out loud or inside her head. Either way she had an odd feeling it came from the fox. She wanted to obey, wanted more than anything to run, but her body refused to listen. Her muscles clenched in terror, in some ancient survival instinct that told her if she didn't move, maybe it wouldn't see her. *Don't run, or it will chase.* She watched, helpless, as the scorpion monster shook off whatever effect the fox's screech had on it and continued to move toward her.

The fox screeched again and dashed between her and the creature, so close she could reach out and touch the fox's vermilion fur—if she was able to move.

The monster backed away again, only a couple steps. Its massive pincer arms rose into the air and snapped in her direction. She stumbled backward, her body finally reacting to the horror in front of her. She dragged her eyes from the scorpion to the fox. It did not turn toward her, merely flicked its tail in agitation.

Liliana turned away from both creatures and did as the fox had told her—she ran. She ran faster and harder than she'd ever run in her life down the trail and back toward her house, toward safety.

She ran and she didn't look back.

<h1 style="text-align:center">11</h1>

Out of breath, heart pounding, Liliana burst through the front door of her house. She went immediately to her parents' bedroom and knocked frantically on the door until she realized no one was inside. She turned and ran outside to her mother's art studio, where she usually was in the mornings. Not bothering to knock, she pushed through the art studio door.

Her mother wasn't there, and her gaze fell on the gift she had painted for her, resting on an easel in the center of the room. Liliana approached it slowly, her eyes wide. The Liliana in the painting was now surrounded by dark smoke and a giant, roughly painted, black scorpion towered over her. Liliana reached out her trembling hand and let her fingertips gently touch the black paint. When she withdrew her hand it was clean—the paint was dry.

Liliana's stomach did a hard flip. It wasn't freshly painted. Her mother added the scorpion long before she'd been attacked.

"No," she whispered, shaking her head in disbelief. "No ..."

She nearly tripped over a mason jar of paint brushes

as she backed out of the studio. She ran back into the house and directly to the bathroom where she slammed and locked the door before falling to her knees in front of the toilet.

Liliana vomited, nothing but hot yellow bile came up from her empty stomach. Horrifying visions flashed in her head of the creature that'd attacked her—its muscled human arms, its dagger tail dripping poison— and of the scorpion in her mother's painting. None of it made sense, she didn't understand why her mother would do that.

She leaned back from the toilet, her eyes red and tearing as sweat streamed down her face. She winced at the bitter, acidic taste of bile left in her mouth. Standing slowly, she flushed the contents of her stomach before going to the sink.

When she looked up she caught her reflection in the mirror and barely recognized herself. Strands of her wavy, dark hair had come loose from her ponytail, her heart-shaped face was glossy with sweat and streaked with dirt. She looked haunted—her brown eyes wide and empty. She stood there, numb, staring at herself in the mirror and struggling to understand what had just happened—what she had just seen.

She felt herself going through the motions of brushing her teeth, taking her clothes off, and getting into the shower. The hot water washed the dirt and sweat away, but it did nothing to clean the memory of the monster or the painting from her mind. In a daze under the steaming water, trying to process what she had seen, she heard Mateo banging on the bathroom door. She couldn't make out what he was saying over the sound of the water but she guessed he needed to use the bathroom. She turned the water off, wrapped herself in a towel, and unlocked the bathroom door. Mateo averted his eyes when he saw her and brushed past her into the bathroom.

"Where's Mom and Dad?" she croaked; her voice strained from sobbing.

"Work. I'm getting a ride with Curtis to school," he replied stiffly as he shut the door in her face.

Liliana walked back to her room and closed the door behind her. She clung to the towel wrapped around her and laid down on her bed. Her hair was dripping wet but she didn't care. She curled herself into a ball, making herself as small as possible. She stared at the wall, not knowing what to do. She wasn't going to school, that much she knew. She wasn't sure if she would ever leave her house again. Crows and visions and whispers were one thing—but being attacked by a half-human, half-scorpion monster was another level. She wished someone would explain to her what was happening, but she didn't even know who to ask.

She flinched at a knock on her door.

"I'm sick!" she yelled. "I'm not going to school today!"

There was a pause, then a muffled voice that didn't belong to anyone in her family replied.

"Liliana?"

She sat up at the sound of Jeremy's voice and forced herself off the bed. She wrapped the towel around her tighter and opened the door an inch.

"What—what are you doing here?" Liliana blurted.

"Your brother let me in. I didn't like how we left things last night," Jeremy said as he ran a hand through his burnt-gold hair. "And then I saw your car was still in the driveway ... I was thinking I could drive you to school today, we could talk ..."

He was looking at her like she was some sort of unpredictable animal. Like she'd be equally likely to bite him as kiss him. Liliana let out a breath. She didn't want to go to school, not after what had just happened. Her hands still trembled and she couldn't see herself going through a normal school day, pretending she wasn't almost eaten by some sort of monstrous atrocity. But Jeremy looked so wounded, so fragile. It hurt her heart to see *him* hurting. *It would be better*, she told herself, *not to be alone. Safety in numbers.*

"Um, okay, hold on, let me get dressed."

She closed the door on Jeremy and got dressed, her hands shaky and her mind moving so fast she couldn't hold onto any of her thoughts. Once decent, she let Jeremy in while she numbly collected her things for school. He prowled around her bedroom like a suspicious cat, watching her movements, studying the things in her room. His eyes fell on the little silver-wrapped gift he'd given her—still unopened—on her desk. He picked it up.

"Oh, I ... I wanted to wait to open it," she stuttered.

Jeremy slowly tore the paper off the box and lifted the lid off. He set the opened gift back on her desk and pulled out a choker-style necklace made of small turquoise stones.

"Come here," he said, and she obeyed.

He unhooked the necklace and put it around her throat, then fastened it at the back of her neck. Her hand flew up to the choker; it was a little uncomfortable, a little too tight, against her sore throat. But she didn't say anything.

She looked at herself in the mirror and tried to smile at Jeremy with her reflection.

"Do you like it?" he asked, one hand resting on the back of her neck where he'd fastened the necklace. She wanted to get away from him, wanted to get out from underneath his surprisingly heavy hand, but she didn't move. She reached up and touched the necklace around her throat.

"Yes, thank you."

They stood that way for a moment, watching each other in the mirror. She squirmed internally until she realized she'd completely forgotten about Ava. She'd be waiting for Liliana to pick her up.

"I have to text Ava!" she said as she slipped out from under Jeremy's grasp. Liliana picked up her phone and winced when she saw the collection of missed texts from her. The last text was Ava telling her she'd gotten a ride from her stepmom instead.

"Oh."

She set the phone inside her tote bag and looked back at Jeremy awkwardly.

"She got a ride from someone else."

"Good, I think I've had about as much of Ava as I can handle for one week." Jeremy said as he turned toward her bedroom door.

Liliana blinked. Jeremy rarely hung out with her friends. Last night's party at his house had been strange—like her two separate worlds were colliding. He didn't have much interest in her friends, but he'd never disparaged them before.

"Come on beautiful, we're going to be late."

Liliana nodded and followed Jeremy out of the house and let him help her up into his Jeep. Her eyes flicked back and forth, searching for a creature that shouldn't exist.

She was distracted on the way to school, nervously looking out the window as if the scorpion monster might appear on a random street corner. The image of the creature was burned into her mind and she couldn't shake it. She wondered if the fox was okay, if it had managed to escape, too. She thought about the words she'd heard in her head—*run, now*—had they really been in her head? They had sounded so foreign, not her own inner voice but someone else's. Could the fox really have spoken to her?

Jeremy reached over and gave her thigh a gentle squeeze and she flinched.

"Geez, so jumpy." He laughed, patting her leg before returning his hand to the steering wheel. She glanced furtively at him; he seemed so calm, so himself. After last night, she was sure he was going to be mad at her for a while, but he acted like nothing had happened. She started to wonder if it had been as bad as she had thought—maybe she had overreacted. It was an eerie feeling, and she wondered if *anything* she experienced lately happened the way she thought it had. It was possible, she considered, that the creature she'd seen in the desert was ...

She shook her head slightly at her own thoughts. There was no mistaking what she had seen. No matter how hard she tried, she couldn't convince herself it'd just been a rabid coyote or a trick of the light. It was real, whatever it was.

And it was still out there.

12

Liliana froze as she entered her first period classroom. A man, far too attractive to be a teacher, was sitting in Mrs. Crane's chair. He looked young—like he was fresh out of college. He was wearing preppy substitute teacher clothes: a white collared shirt under a brown blazer and khaki pants. His hair was the color of late autumn, a deep red with gold highlights.

He turned to look at her and everything inside of her went still. His eyes were an impossible color, but so familiar. They were the shade of wildflower honey, a warm glowing amber. And they were locked onto *her*.

"Who are you?" she whispered, dazed. She felt like she knew him, and yet she was certain she'd never seen him before.

"I'm Mr. Reynard," he replied smoothly, rising to his feet. Her head tipped upward as he stood, looming above her. The scent of campfire smoke and pine wafted off of him. She realized her mouth was slightly open and shut it.

"I'm filling in for Mrs. Crane, she's out sick. Now, if you'll take your seat?"

Liliana nodded dumbly and moved down the rows

of desks to her seat. Every other student was already at their desks and she felt exposed as they watched her sit down. The seat in front of hers was empty, giving her a clear view of the strange man with amber eyes. He wandered around Mrs. Crane's desk, flipping through papers until he found what he was looking for. He glanced up from the paper, his eyes moving over the students, then set the paper back on the desk.

Liliana couldn't take her eyes off the man as he casually paced at the front of the room. He launched into a lecture about Greek mythology, for some reason, ignoring the copies of *Wuthering Heights* on everyone's desks and the lesson plan she was sure Mrs. Crane must have left for him.

"The five rivers of the underworld," he was saying, "are Styx, Lethe, Acheron, Phlegethon, and Cocytus. The river Styx is the most well-known. I'm certain you have all at least heard of it before?"

He paused and about half of the class nodded their heads. Liliana did not. She'd studied Greek mythology her sophomore year like everyone else had, but they'd just read *The Odyssey,* and she barely remembered it.

"The Styx is the primary river of the underworld. The ferryman Charon takes souls across it from the land of the living to the land of the dead."

Liliana swallowed, her throat still sore. She didn't understand why this strange substitute teacher was going on about underworld rivers. She shifted uncomfortably in her seat and eyed the clock above the teacher's head. She didn't want to hear any more of this. Didn't want to think about death any more.

"The Lethe is the river of forgetfulness," he continued. "Souls drink from this river to forget their past life. Acheron is the river of woe, or misery. Phlegethon is the river of fire. It leads to Tartarus where souls are judged. And Cocytus—" he paused briefly, his piercing eyes shifting to Liliana, "—is the river of wailing. There are different ideas about Cocytus. Some say when Charon refuses to ferry a soul over, it is forced to remain on the banks of Cocytus. Others say it was the river where murderers were punished."

Liliana sat back in her chair; her face hot for a reason she couldn't understand. *Why is he looking at me like that?*

"Nice," a boy a few seats away said. Mr. Reynard ignored him, and continued to talk about the underworld, but Liliana stopped listening. All she could think about was that last river—where murderers were punished—and the way Mr. Reynard looked at her.

The rest of the class went by in a blur and she was surprised when the bell rang. Her fellow students moved almost as one up from their seats and flowed out the front door. A couple of the girls paused to talk to Mr. Reynard, bending down in front of him in grossly obvious displays of cleavage. Liliana hovered, hoping the girls would hurry up and leave so she could talk to him alone. She didn't know what she was going to say, but felt a strong pull toward the man with dark-red hair and amber eyes. She felt like he had something, something she needed.

Finally, the girls left and Liliana approached him, studying his face as he in turn studied her.

"I—"

"Liliana." She felt her name on the back of her neck, a firm coldness in the tone. Her body tensed as she turned to see Jeremy looming above her, his jaw tight and his eyes flashing. She'd forgotten Jeremy had English second period; she rarely ran into him between classes. Normally, she'd be half-way across campus by now to get to her science class. Today, though, she lingered.

"You're going to be late to your next class," Jeremy continued, his tone low and serious. Jeremy's eyes flicked to Mr. Reynard then back to her. He took her by the arm and hurried her toward the door.

"Liliana," Mr. Reynard practically purred her name, causing her cheeks to warm. She pulled away from Jeremy and turned back towards the substitute teacher. He smirked and held out a folded piece of paper. She looked down at it, confused. His amber eyes were intense, his tone firm and a little commanding. "Your assignment."

Liliana took the paper mechanically, not understanding what he was talking about. *What assignment? Did I miss something?* She shoved the paper into her bag and rushed from the classroom, brushing past Jeremy. She was careful not to catch his eye, didn't want to see the glare she was certain he'd be giving her. With a heaviness in her chest, she half-ran to her next class. Jeremy had *just* forgiven her for the night before, they were good again, and she'd screwed it up already.

She felt jittery as she entered the science room but was relieved to see Mr. Henderson at the front of the class and not another replacement. She sat down on her stool and tried to avoid meeting Killian's glare across the table from her. She thought about how he had stormed out the day before, in a huff about ... Liliana struggled to remember what had happened. Something she had said upset him, but she couldn't remember what it was. She internally shrugged and decided she didn't care. Killian and his drama were the least important things in her life right now.

"Scorpions!" Mr. Henderson's voice bellowed from the front of the classroom and Liliana's whole body tensed. She whipped around to look at her teacher. He set a large glass jar on the long table that served as his desk. She was too far away to see what was inside of it, but she had a bad feeling she knew what it was.

"Ticks!" Mr. Henderson continued as he placed a much smaller jar next to the first one.

"Spiders!" he called out, placing a third jar on the table.

He had everyone's undivided attention now.

"What do these three creatures have in common?" the teacher asked, looking out at the class.

"They're all disgusting?" Helsie called out in response. A few light laughs followed.

"Well, that's a matter of opinion," Mr. Henderson said. "Anyone else? What do spiders, scorpions, and ticks all have in common?"

A hand went up tentatively.

"Yes, Greg?"

"They all live in the desert?"

Mr. Henderson nodded, albeit a bit begrudgingly.

"Yes, that's true. What else?"

Across from her Killian raised one skinny, ghost-pale arm in the air. Mr. Henderson nodded in his direction.

"They are all arachnids," Killian answered in a growl, as if he had been forced to answer instead of volunteering. Liliana rolled her eyes.

"Yes!" Mr. Henderson practically yelped, his face brightening. "They are all in the arachnid family. Now," Mr. Henderson pulled down the screen rolled up above the whiteboard, "we're going to watch this short documentary on arachnids. Tina, can you hit the lights for me, please?"

The lights went out and Liliana found herself clutching the edge of the table, much like she had at dinner the night before. The projector clicked on from somewhere on the ceiling and the documentary started to play.

She found herself paying more attention to the video than she had anything in that class all year. She thought about the abomination she'd seen in the desert that morning, the horror show of half-scorpion and half-human freak of nature. This documentary wasn't going to cover the creature she'd seen, but still …

She jotted down notes any time she heard something potentially useful about scorpions. The act of list-making calmed her, and her mind began to feel clearer.

Hunt at night. Eight legs. Can live on one insect a year. Different kinds of scorpions have different kinds of venom. Venom is used to subdue prey, self-defense, and in some species, mating. Causes paralysis and death.

Liliana stared down at her notes in the dim room. Reading them back it just seemed like a bunch of random, useless information. She read her notes over and over, trying to glean something useful from them, and ignored the rest of the video as it moved on to spiders and ticks.

The lights came on and Liliana blinked against the sudden brightness. She'd been so focused on the list in front of her that she hadn't even noticed the documentary had ended.

The bell rang and she shoved her notebook back into her bag, her eyes catching on a loose piece of folded paper. The "assignment" Mr. Reynard had given her. She shook her head in disbelief that she'd forgotten about it.

She pulled out the paper and read what he had scrawled in heavy black pen.

It's going to get worse.

* * *

Liliana spent the next two classes staring at the one sentence Mr. Reynard had written on the piece of paper he'd given her. *It's going to get worse.*

She couldn't understand why a teacher would write that. She realized, too, that she couldn't be sure what he was talking about. There were so many things that could get worse. She thought of the monster that had attacked her that morning. It felt like an odd, fuzzy memory, like a nightmare she'd had and partially forgotten, but still sensed floating around at the back of her mind.

She needed to talk to Mr. Reynard; she knew that much. When the lunch bell rang, she hurried across campus toward her English classroom. She prayed he was still there and hadn't left already for his own lunch break.

As Liliana moved through the open-air quad, whispers surrounded her, assaulting her ears. These whispers, though, weren't in her head. They were coming from the students around her. There was an odd quiet, a tension in the air she'd never felt before. A sick feeling crept through her—something was wrong. The classroom was visible just across the quad, she was so close to getting some answers about what was happening to her. But the anxious whispering, the electricity in the air—she had to find her friends. She needed to make sure everyone was okay.

Reluctantly, she changed direction and headed to the cafeteria instead. She found her friends at their usual table—Ruby, Diego, and Ava were already there, the same whispers tainting their lips.

"What?" Liliana asked as she sat next to Ava. "What is going on?"

Ava opened her mouth, then shut it and looked over at Ruby.

"Isabel is dead." Ruby said softly as she tilted her head towards Ben, Isabel's boyfriend, a few tables away from them. "He just found out."

Ben was a mess—his long, dusty brown hair disheveled, his eyes bloodshot. He'd taken off his glasses and the hand he was holding them with was trembling. He was shaking his head, saying the same words over and over as his friends surrounded him.

"I should have walked her home, I offered ... I should have walked her home ... why didn't I just walk her home?"

A jolt ran through Liliana that spread through her body and limbs like static electricity underneath her skin. She had known someone was going to die—was this what she had felt?

"How—" Liliana's voice cracked under the question, "—how did she die?" Liliana felt sick, images from news stories flooding her mind. The things that happened to girls alone at night.

"Some sort of animal attack," Ruby answered, leaning closer to her to whisper the words. "Someone found her on the sidewalk just a block away from her house. She'd been at Ben's and was walking home—but she never made it there. I heard—" Ruby paused, looking around them to make sure no one was listening, then lowered her voice even further, "parts of her were just *gone. Eaten.*"

"*Mierda,*" Liliana whispered, her stomach turning at the thought of poor Isabel. She'd just talked to her yesterday—she'd been so eager and Liliana had blown her off. And now she was dead.

Dead. Liliana thought of the vision she'd had last night, of being inside some other girl's body. She pulled at the memory, recalled her bitten-down fingernails, her straight, silky hair. How skinny and uncoordinated she'd been. The flip flops.

Her skin prickled as she realized what it was she saw, experienced—it was Isabel. It was Isabel's *death*. She didn't see what killed her, just felt the fear as Isabel ran from it, the burning pain in her back before she woke up on Jeremy's deck.

"What, ah, what kind of animal do they think it

was?" Liliana thought about the scorpion monster she'd run into in the desert. She got away, but maybe Isabel wasn't so lucky.

Ruby shrugged as her dark eyes slipped back over to Ben's hunched figure. Diego wrapped an arm around Ruby and pulled her closer to him. Usually, Ruby would have pushed Diego away, annoyed with the public display of affection, annoyed by his closeness. But today she didn't.

Liliana scanned the cafeteria nervously. She realized she hadn't seen Jeremy since that morning. It'd just been a few hours, but ...

"Has anyone seen Jeremy?" she asked, an irrational panic straining her voice. She looked frantically around the bustling cafeteria.

"There," Ava said, pointing at a table at the far end of the room. Liliana followed Ava's finger and locked eyes with Jeremy. He was staring right at her, surrounded by his friends but ignoring them completely. He wasn't smiling. A chill ran through her and then he turned away. He'd never looked at her like that before, with such anger. Such coldness. She considered going over there to talk to him, but the thought was interrupted by an eruption of whispers inside her head. She'd had a few blissful, quiet hours, but now the voices were back.

Twenty years, three months, five days. She recognized this voice, like squeaking wheels and beeping monitors.

Three years, four months, nine days. A new voice, the sound of glass smashing.

One year, two months, three days. A voice like gunfire.

More and more voices crowded her, demanding

attention. Without thinking she covered her ears with her hands and shut her eyes tightly. *Stop, please stop.*

The voices refused to listen, instead growing in volume, no longer soft whispers but screams. Her throat felt raw and ached. The choker Jeremy had put on her that morning was too tight. She tried to get the clasp unhooked, tears collected in her eyes as she frantically tried to get the necklace off her swelling throat.

"Get it off!" she gasped out as she tore at her neck. "Get it off!"

Ava's cool hands were against the back of her neck. Liliana exhaled as she felt the tightness of the choker loosen and fall away. She rubbed at her sore throat; the pain only slightly lessened by the removal of the necklace.

The voices grew louder, more demanding, and Liliana didn't know what to do. Her heart raced, her face slick with sweat. One voice pushed itself above the others, so loud she thought her eardrums might burst. A deafening roar of a crackling fire. Dirt crunching underneath boots.

Ten hours.

She couldn't take it anymore, couldn't hold herself together any longer. She opened her mouth and screamed.

13

Liliana opened her eyes and was hit by a wave of heat coming off of the large bonfire in front of her. She looked up, the sky was dark except for a scattering of stars and the gray smoke billowing up from the fire. Around her were various kids from school, some she recognized and some she didn't with cans of beer in their hands. She felt...different. Her body wasn't her body. The person she was inside looked down and she was able to see her breasts were gone, replaced with a flat, muscled chest, and she felt something in her pants that definitely wasn't there before.

Ay dios mío, I'm a guy.

She got up from the rock she'd been sitting on, though it wasn't her telling the body to move. Like last time, she couldn't control this body, either. She tried to memorize every detail of where she was, who she was with. She was at a party somewhere out in the desert, that much was obvious, but where? The body moved further away from the warmth of the fire, away from the yelling voices. *Oh, no, where am I going?*

She then realized she felt an uncomfortable pressure on her bladder. *His* bladder.

I have to pee, oh God I really don't want to see this!

She walked behind a particularly large saguaro and felt his hands unzip his jeans. The acrid smell of urine hit her senses and she felt like she might puke. Someone behind him said something, but it sounded strange, like an echo. The voice said more, but she couldn't understand the words.

"What?" he called over his shoulder at the unknown speaker. The body wavered back and forth slightly as he stopped urinating and zipped up his jeans. She heard a familiar hissing sound behind him, and Liliana knew what was about to happen.

She tried to force the body to listen to her, to move, to *run*, but she was just a visitor.

"Okay, what—" the boy grumbled as he slowly turned around. There was a flash of color and then the scorpion man's dagger tail was in motion, slicing through the boy's clothes, his skin, as it buried itself deep in his chest. She felt the boy's confusion, then his pain. The poison rushed into her body and burned inside her veins, moving through her like a river of searing lava. The boy's body crumpled to the ground and the fire in her veins went out as he released his last breath.

14

Liliana opened her eyes and squinted at the blinding fluorescent light above her.

That's the second time I've died, she thought numbly. She could still feel an echo of the pain, of the burning running through her veins.

Slowly, she sat up and looked around the small room. She was on a long, cushioned bench and her tote bag was slumped over on a nearby blue plastic chair. The walls were covered with ancient-looking medical posters yellowed and curled at the edges. One had a pair of lungs on it, one side red and the other black. THIS IS WHAT HAPPENS TO YOUR LUNGS WHEN YOU SMOKE was written in large, bold black letters across the top. A newer-looking poster next to it had an illustration of a girl with string attached to her limbs in grotesque puppetry. DON'T BE VAPING'S PUPPET it yelled in all caps. *That one doesn't even make sense,* she thought with an eye roll.

She'd never been in the school nurse's office before, and being there now, alone, made her feel itchy. She searched her mind for a memory of how she had gotten there but found nothing. The last thing she remembered was being in the cafeteria with her friends, and then—

The desert at night, wandering through cacti, the pain in her chest. Was it something that had already happened, or something that was waiting in the future? She hugged herself and rubbed her hands up and down her arms. She felt strange, like the skin of the person she'd been inside still covered her.

"Oh, you're awake," an overly bubbly voice chirped from the doorway. The young nurse grinned broadly, her blonde hair in a ponytail and her eyes bright blue and wide. She smiled and held out a dusty-looking box of cookies and an apple juice box. Liliana absentmindedly took both; she didn't know what else to do.

"For your blood sugar," the nurse gestured at the food items in Liliana's hands.

"My ... blood sugar?"

"Probably why you fainted, low blood sugar. Happens all the time." The nurse smiled and revealed perfectly white, orthodontia-crafted teeth. Liliana pictured the woman popping her retainer in at night, like she had to do.

"Ah, thanks, but I feel okay now." Liliana set the juice and cookies next to her on the bench.

"I'd feel a lot better if you at least drank the juice." The nurse made her eyes somehow wider and Liliana was reminded of a pouting cartoon cat. She picked up the apple juice and took the plastic wrapper off the straw, then stabbed it into the small hole at the top of the box. She took three strong sucks and emptied the small juice box.

The nurse smiled and took the empty container from her.

"You know, I rarely get any real medical problems." The nurse said with a wry smile. "Usually it's just kids faking sick, or period cramps, or someone just trying to get out of class for a while."

Liliana stared at the pretty blonde nurse and wondered why she was telling her this. She eyed the door and started to plan her great escape.

"Well, I'm better now, so—"

Twenty years, four months, five days.

The whisper came to her stronger than ever before, the usual chorus of voices quiet except for this one. The voice was a thudding sound, rhythmic and hollow. *Thump, thump, thump.*

"Did you drive to school today?" the nurse asked, her expression a practiced calm. Liliana shook away the thudding voice and met the nurse's crystal blue eyes.

"N-no, my boyfriend drove me."

"That's probably for the best. Don't want you blacking out while driving. Is there someone I can call to come pick you up? Your mom?"

Liliana thought about the ruined painting in her mom's studio. She didn't know where her mother was, and wasn't sure she was ready to face her. She thought about what she had told her last night about her abuela.

"No, she's working," Liliana lied, "can you call my grandma?"

"Of course, as long as she's on the approved pickup list ..." The nurse went over to a small computer, to look her up in the system, she assumed.

"I'm eighteen, my birthday was yesterday, does that really still apply?"

"Um ..." The nurse looked around the room as if someone with more experience might suddenly appear to save her from Liliana's question. "... I ...guess not?"

Before the nurse could offer to check with someone—like the frog-mouthed secretary that clearly hated all of the students—Liliana stood up from the bench and grabbed her bag.

"Great, I can call her myself. I'll wait for her outside."

Liliana sat down on a shaded bench in the front of the school. She pulled her phone out of her bag and unlocked it. Scrolling through her recent calls, she felt a pinch of guilt when she didn't see her abuela's number pop up. *I really should call her more*, Liliana chastised herself. She found her number in her contacts and pushed the call button.

She listened as it rang once, twice, then a click.

"*¿Quien murió?*" Her abuela's tense voice hit her. *Who died?*

Liliana was about to say no one, then remembered poor Isabel. But Isabel wasn't who her abuela was asking about.

"*Todo está bien*, I just need someone to pick me up from school, I'm not feeling well."

There was an oddly long pause on the other end of the line and she wondered what her grandmother was considering so carefully.

"Unless you're busy..."

"No, no, I'll come to get you. *Diez minutos.*" Click.

Twenty minutes later her grandmother's beaten-up red pick up truck pulled up and lurched to a stop in front of her. She stood from the bench and walked over, pulling hard on the door handle as she knew she'd have to, and yanked the sticky door open. She stepped up and sat down on the warm, worn-out brown leather seats, covered with thin white scratches and a few larger tears. The truck had the faint grassy smell of horses.

She clicked the seat belt on and looked at her grandmother sitting in the driver's seat. She was wearing faded blue jeans in the same condition as the truck's seats and a hot pink tank top Liliana thought was a little too low cut for someone her age. Her long, gray hair was wrapped into a bun on top of her head.

"*Gracias Abuela*," Liliana said as she clutched her tote bag in her lap. "For picking me up."

Her grandmother stared back at her and Liliana squirmed under the old woman's calculating gaze.

"Why didn't you call Violeta?"

Violeta. It was always weird when she heard her mother's name. She was always just Mami or Mamá at home.

"I—I wanted to talk to you about something." Liliana replied, not really knowing where to start.

Her grandmother didn't take her eyes off the road but nodded, more to herself than Liliana, it seemed.

"Okay," she said, a shadow of a sigh in her voice. "Let's talk."

* * *

At her grandmother's small ranch, Liliana tried to relax. On the back porch the comforting smell of hay and horses wafted over from the stalls. Plants grew all around them in large pots—desert-honeysuckle with burnt-orange tubular flowers, bushy chuparosa with bright scarlet blossoms. They sat together on a worn wooden bench and both tilted their heads at the same time to watch a tiny jewel-feathered hummingbird flit from flower to flower.

"So, *mi lirio,* was there something you wanted to ask me?"

Liliana's eyes darted to her grandmother, whose attention was on a ruby-throated hummingbird flitting its wings on a nearby branch.

"I—I don't know."

Sitting there with her grandmother, surrounded by tiny birds and fire-colored flowers, everything she'd experienced earlier started to feel more like a bad dream than reality. *This* was real, not the whispers and visions. Not the monsters.

She thought of Isabel's anxious face, her straight hair and big hopeful eyes. Liliana tried to remember what she had said to her yesterday outside of class but it was foggy, she'd barely been paying attention. What she did remember was how dismissive of Isabel she had been. Now Isabel was dead—and as much as she didn't want to believe it, she had *experienced* Isabel's death.

Liliana had been there when she died. Had been *inside* of her. Had died with her. Now it had happened again.

She took a deep breath to ease the tightness in her chest. She struggled with what she should say to her grandmother. Death visions, scorpion monsters, her mother's ruined painting. It all felt like too much, and she didn't know where to begin. She remembered her mother's odd expression last night, how she'd spoken so cryptically about her abuela's dead roses and their own dying walnut tree. It felt like a safe place to start.

"When my mom was my age," she started slowly, not sure where she was going with this or what sort of answer she'd get, "she said all your rose bushes died."

Liliana eyed her grandmother's side profile, the old woman's eyes still chasing hummingbirds. She watched for a reaction, but her abuela's face was blank.

"She ... she said you weren't surprised," Liliana continued uncertainly. "Why weren't you surprised?"

Her grandmother licked her dry, cracked lips and finally moved her head to look at Liliana.

"Ah, *por supuesto*. That. I'm going to need a drink."

Liliana's grandmother got up from the bench and disappeared inside the house. She hesitated, unsure if she was suppose to follow her grandmother. A moment later she reappeared, a pair of perspiring glass bottles in her hands. She handed a root beer to Liliana and sat back down beside her. She took a long drink from her own bottle—a real beer instead of the sugary non-alcoholic drink Liliana now held in her hands.

"Okay, to tell you about the roses I first have to tell you about Maria."

"Maria? Who—"

"Hush and I'll tell you," Liliana's abuela shot her an annoyed look and took another drink from her beer. "Long ago, there was a woman called Maria. She was very beautiful, very vain, and very foolish. She married the wrong man—he, too, was beautiful, vain, and foolish. They had two children together and were briefly happy, but soon her handsome husband showed his true face. It was an ugly face, full of anger and disgust for Maria. He blamed her for everything that went wrong."

Liliana waited awkwardly in the pause, uncertain if she should speak. Her grandmother's eyes looked off into the distance, she was somewhere else completely. She ran her tongue quickly across her chapped lips and continued her story.

"He hit Maria until she was no longer beautiful, and then left. He would return every few months to see the children, but refused to speak to Maria, to even look at her. One day her husband brought another woman with him to visit. Maria watched from inside her house as her husband and his new wife played with her children. Something inside of her snapped watching them like that. She was consumed with the thought that her husband and his new wife would take her children away and leave her all alone and she would never see him—or her children—again."

Liliana didn't like where this story was going. It sounded vaguely familiar, like an old ghost story she'd heard as a child.

"That night Maria drowned her two children in the nearby river, then herself."

Liliana cringed. She had expected the dark ending, but it still hit harshly in her ears.

Her grandmother let out a long breath and turned to look at Liliana.

"A day later one of her children, the girl, came back

out of the water."

A chill ran through Liliana as a dream she had forgotten came back to her. She remembered a beautiful woman trying to drown her in the bloody river. *You never should have come out of the water.*

"She returned to her mother's house," her abuela continued. "And acted as if nothing had happened. The next night the wailing began. All night a loud, ear-piercing crying from the bank of the river. When people came to see what the sound was they saw Maria, her long hair matted and dirty, her face pale and her eyes just black holes in her head. She walked the riverbank crying, and they soon understood her words. *¿Dónde está mi hija?* She would scream, over and over, until the sun rose and she disappeared back into the water. Every night was spent this way, looking for the daughter that lived when she should have died. Soon her real name was forgotten and she was known only as La Llorona—the Weeping Woman."

Liliana rubbed at her arms, cold despite the hot sun overhead. She recognized the story now. She'd heard a different version as a child, but she remembered the name.

"Every child knows the story of La Llorona," her grandmother continued, as if hearing Liliana's thoughts. "But no one—no one but *us*—knows the story of her daughter, Faustina. Faustina is your great-great-great-grandmother."

Liliana's mouth slid open slightly, her eyes squinting in confusion and disbelief. "No, that doesn't—that's just a ghost story to scare children into behaving. It's not real." What she experienced was just a dream. Nothing more.

Her grandmother shook her head sadly and continued.

"Faustina came back from the water changed. Nothing grew around her, all the vegetables in her mother's garden died. A darkness spread itself out around her and the townspeople avoided her. Then the children of the village began to go missing, only to be found dead on the riverbank. Faustina was no fool, she could feel the townspeople's eyes on her. She knew they would always fear her, always see her as the daughter of La Llorona, and that soon they would come for her. She left that town in the middle of the night and never returned."

Her grandmother paused to take another drink from her beer, then set the now empty bottle on a side table. Liliana looked down at her own root beer, still full.

"I don't understand, what does this have to do with your dead roses?"

"The daughters of La Llorona are all touched by death," her grandmother answered. "Faustina paid some terrible price to return from the river. Her ancestors—*we*—will continue to pay it. It happened to me at your age, your mother, my mother, every woman as far back as Faustina. It's always the same—but always different. It always seems to start with the death of surrounding plants. Like when Faustina returned to her home from the river. My roses, your mother's walnut tree."

Liliana didn't dare look at her grandmother. She didn't want to disrespect her but everything she said was impossible. Crazy. Liliana shook her head.

"The curse will get worse," her grandmother said with no emotion in her voice. "And then it will be gone."

"Gone?" Liliana blurted. *Gone!* It was more than she had hoped for. Relief rushed through her as she soaked in the information. Whatever was happening to her—the curse as her abuela called it—would *end*. She just had to stay strong until then. *I can do that*, she thought firmly.

"When will it be over?" she asked, trying to calm the excitement in her voice. "Why didn't you warn me? Why didn't Mamá?"

"Your mother never believed the story, she ... made herself forget, I think. I had hoped that maybe the curse would end with your mother, maybe you would be spared. *Pero no*. I don't know when it will stop—or why it comes and goes. Could be a week or a month, but no longer than a year."

A year. Liliana felt the blood rush from her face. That's not at all what she was hoping to hear. She wanted something to look forward to, a certainty that this would indeed end—and *soon*.

"Come, I have to water the horses." Her grandmother stood up with a soft groan and started down the path to the back gate which led to the horse stalls. Liliana stayed seated, still reeling from what she had just learned. She set her untouched root beer down next to the empty beer bottle and hurried after her grandmother, a thousand questions clamoring around inside her head.

Liliana followed her grandmother into the stable, a large cream-colored structure with two sides of horse stalls. Her grandmother had it built a few years ago, and was almost nicer than her actual house. Inside, her grandmother turned on the water and pulled the heavy rubber hose loose from its holder. Liliana drifted distractedly behind as her grandmother filled the buckets hanging on the inside of the stalls.

"So, what does your curse look like?" her grandmother muttered, not looking at Liliana but focused on the rising water level of the bucket she was filling.

"What do you mean?"

"How does death communicate with you?" her grandmother clarified. "It's never the same. The messages came to your mother through her paintings. It terrified her, it terrified all of us. She would paint these horrific murder scenes ... and then of course, they would come true."

Liliana thought about her mother's painting ruined with the sloppily-painted black scorpion. She considered telling her abuela about the painting, but it felt like she'd be betraying her mother, somehow.

"What about you?" Liliana asked instead.

"I was lucky, I suppose," her grandmother said with a sigh. "I would see—little messages, in things. It's hard to explain. I'd look at a rock, say, and would see words within the cracks. Locations, always locations, that's all. I thought I was going crazy."

Liliana's brows pinched together as she considered this. Her mother saw the how, her grandmother saw the where.

I hear the when.

"I hear voices," Liliana finally answered. "They all

just say time—like, five years, one month, two days. I think—I think it's the time left before the person dies."

Her grandmother looked at her, surprised. "Voices? Are you hearing them right now?"

Liliana knew what her grandmother was asking.

"I ... they come and go," she answered. "I'm getting better at sort of, blocking them out."

There was a long silence, and then, "Can you hear—do you know when I am going to die?" Her grandmother didn't even stop to look at her when she asked. Liliana could hear her grandmother's death whisper. She wasn't sure if she wanted to know, but as she concentrated the voice became clearer, louder.

"I can." She sent the voice back, lost it in the otherworldly chorus of voices. "Do you—do you want to know?"

Her grandmother didn't lift her gaze from the hose. The wrinkles in her face looked deeper, her eyes tired.

"Of course, I do," she replied with a shrug. "And of course, I don't."

Liliana nodded. She didn't want to know when her grandmother would die—then again, it might be better to be prepared instead of taken by surprise. She let the voice stay where it was, far enough away to be indecipherable. Liliana felt a soft nudge on her shoulder and looked up to see one of her grandmother's horses, a dappled gray mare named Sunshine, staring at her with big, dark eyes. She smiled and ran her hand along the horse's soft cheek. The horse huffed out a breath that smelled like carrots. She let her hand slip away from the horse and turned back to her grandmother, already making her way to the next stall.

"I've also been getting these ... these ... *visions*."

This made her grandmother stop abruptly between stalls and Liliana almost crashed into her.

"Visions? In addition to the voices?"

Liliana looked at her grandmother with concern. "Yeah, I mean, is that not ..."

"Tell me about these visions."

So, Liliana did. She told her about her sore throat, Isabel, experiencing her death. How she knew another death was coming—the boy in the desert. She left out, however, the monstrous scorpion creature that was doing the killing, that had attacked her that morning. She knew she should tell her grandmother about the monster, but Liliana didn't know how she would react. She was afraid her grandmother would freak out, lock her in her room to keep her safe. Liliana couldn't be trapped inside her house right now. She needed to help this boy.

"I didn't understand what was happening the first time, with Isabel, but I know now. I have to find a way to stop the next death. I have to save this boy, whoever he is." Liliana finished, eyes shining. "I can stop it from happening again."

Her grandmother gave her a pitying look and patted her on the arm.

"Stop it? Oh, *mi lirio*, you can't *stop* it."

15

Liliana stared at the faded green star stickers on her ceiling. Her grandmother's words echoed in her head like a taunt. *You can't stop it.*

She was relieved when her grandmother had dropped her off at home and no one was there. Her brother wasn't back from school yet, her parents were still out. She didn't know how to ask her mother about the painting or if her mother even realized what she'd done—or what it could mean.

Her phone dinged for what must have been the twentieth time in the last two hours. She groaned irritably. She was ignoring it, not wanting to face the onslaught of questions from her friends—from Jeremy. She reached for it anyway and sighed as she scrolled through her missed texts. Most of them were from Ava and Jeremy, one from Ruby, and one from her mother asking her to order a pizza for dinner as she would be out late at a gallery show and her father had to drive out of town to examine some sick pigs. Then a text from Helsie popped up. Liliana was surprised to see Helsie's name; she forgot she even had Helsie saved in her phone. It was clearly a group text, Liliana saw the long list of numbers the message had been sent to.

Party at the wash tonight. BYOB.

Liliana scowled at the message and set the phone face down next to her on the bed. *A party?* She couldn't believe they were throwing a party after what had just happened to Isabel.

Liliana shook her head. It'd been awhile since she bothered going to parties at the wash. It was just a spot in one of the dry riverbeds running through the foothills, hidden from the prying eyes of adults. They were usually pretty lame and always had way more guys than girls. Someone always ended up puking. Someone always fell into a cactus. It'd grown old fast for her.

The vision she had at lunch flashed through her mind. The boy she was inside, who died, was at a party in the desert when it happened. Liliana eyed the text. *What if it is this party?*

It was the last thing she wanted to do.

Her bedroom door flew open and she jumped, dropping her phone on the hard tile. She winced at the loud clatter it made. She glared at Mateo, standing in her doorway with a *oops* face on. He picked the phone up and handed it to her. "It's fine, these things are indestructible."

"Mm." She examined her phone, he was right, it was undamaged.

"Mamá said you're ordering pizza for dinner," Mateo said.

Liliana stared back. "Yeah, so?"

"So .... do it."

Liliana rolled her eyes.

"Fine. Pineapple and anchovies, right?"

Mateo made a face and crossed his arms.

When the pizza came they ate it in silence, her brother with his face in a book and Liliana glued to her phone. She was texting with Ava and Ruby about the party, trying to convince them to go with her. There was no way she was going to a wash party alone. After a little badgering they agreed.

A couple hours later Ruby pulled up to her house in her mom's black Range Rover, Diego in the front seat and Ava in the back. Liliana got in and slid into the empty seat next to Ava. Ruby eyed her in the rearview mirror. "So, are we going to talk about why Jeremy isn't coming with us?"

Liliana didn't respond, staring out the window as they drove to the wash. Jeremy wouldn't be happy that she went to this party without him, but she was afraid he would talk her out of going.

They parked behind a long string of cars and walked down the familiar dirt trail that led down to the wash. Liliana could hear voices echoing up from the dry riverbed. She followed the trail as it zigzagged down to the bottom where a bonfire was already raging.

Whoever had built the fire had made it way too large, the branches and wood logs piled too high. They'd be lucky if the party lasted an hour before someone came and broke it up.

Kids from her high school were scattered around the bonfire in small groups of two, three, and four. She recognized some of them, others she didn't. A couple guys who looked a few years out of high school eyed a group of three younger girls, sophomores, Liliana guessed. The girls stood close together, eyes doe-wide. They were all staring at a red cooler, clearly wanting what was inside but too afraid to grab one, or ask. It was a boy Liliana was here to protect, but she would keep an eye on those girls, too.

Ruby and Diego went to talk to someone they knew, leaving her with Ava. Ava pulled her coat tighter around her against the brisk night air and watched Liliana suspiciously.

"Cold? Want to move closer to the fire?" Liliana asked, hoping to distract Ava from whatever her thoughts were.

"No. Lili, why are we here?" Ava's voice was soft, gentle. "I hate these parties. *You* hate these parties."

Liliana didn't know how to answer her. She couldn't tell her the truth, and she hadn't thought to come up with a lie.

"I ... just needed to get out," she said, lamely. She hoped Ava would let it go.

"Mm," Ava said, unconvinced. "I'm here, you know? If you need to ... talk about anything. About ... Jeremy .... or ..."

Liliana turned her full attention to Ava. "Jeremy? Why would I need to talk about Jeremy?"

Ava looked away from her and toward the fire. "I just ... he just doesn't seem like a very good boyfriend."

Liliana shook her head. Jeremy might not be perfect, but he *was* a good boyfriend. She was the one avoiding him, ruining his birthday plans for her. She felt guilty then, being at this party without him. Intentionally leaving him out. Her body tensed as she thought about what he would say to her when he found out she'd come here without him. She tried to push the thought from her mind, tried to focus on why she was at the party to start with.

Liliana's eyes moved over every person at the party, sizing them up, cataloging them in her mind. She focused on the boys.

Finn was there with Helsie; they were entwined, making out against a boulder. There were a handful of guys she didn't recognize at all, uncertain they even went to her school. There were the three older guys eyeing the sophomore girls. A short distance away, apart from everyone else, was a human-shaped shadow— *Killian?*

She'd never seen Killian at any parties before, was pretty sure he didn't even have any friends. But here he was, at *this* party. He was smoking a cigarette a little away from everyone else, staring at the bonfire's flickering flames. He wore a black sweatshirt with the hood pulled up over his head and baggy torn-up jeans. She took a step toward him, then thought better of it. Killian made it clear he hated her, and some small part of her didn't really care if he was the one who died tonight.

Guilt blew through her at the thought, and she hated herself for feeling that way. She didn't want Killian to die, but she couldn't fight the feeling that if *someone* had to die, he wasn't the *worst* option.

Killian turned away from the fire and locked eyes with her, as if he could hear her thoughts. She turned away and saw that the three older guys had approached the girls they'd been watching. The girls now had cans of beer in their hands and were giggling nervously. Liliana watched as the guys moved their bodies between the girls and the rest of the party, slowly pushing the girls away from the rest of the group, into the darkness of the desert.

Hot fury rushed through her.

She stalked over to the group and slid between the girls and the guys. One of the men sized her up and grinned, revealing tobacco-stained teeth.

"Hey sweetheart," he drawled, already drunk. "You want to come with us? We're going—"

"I don't care where you're going!" she snapped, a surge of hate and disgust flooding her, blinding her.

She turned her back on the guys and directed her attention to the three sophomore girls. Up close they looked even younger than she had thought—they were *babies.*

"These," Liliana gestured vaguely at the men behind her, "are what we call disgusting creepers. Don't go anywhere with them, and certainly don't drink anything they give you." She took the cans from the girls' hands and dumped the contents into the dry dirt.

"Hey!" the guys called out in near unison behind her. She whipped around to face them. Two of the guys stepped back and looked everywhere but at her. The other, the leader of this trio of douchebags she assumed, stood his ground. He towered above her short frame, and she was repulsed by his glazed-over eyes and smirking mouth. She wanted to slap him.

"You," she directed at the man in front of her, "need to leave. Unless you want me to call the cops? Tell them you're giving underage girls alcohol?"

The man scoffed and looked over her head at the girls cowering behind her. He took a deep drink from his beer then tossed the can out into the desert.

"They're ugly anyway," he spat. One of the girls behind her let out a pained gasp. He jerked his head, and his two friends followed him as he left the party. Liliana watched as they scrambled up the trail out of the wash. She let out a breath and turned back around.

"You're *not* ugly—and don't be so stupid," she snapped at them, erasing the look of admiration they all had painted on their faces. "There's not always going to be someone to save you, get it?"

The girls nodded and looked down at the ground, at the fallen cans of beer. Liliana wanted to tell them to go home, but she didn't know where those guys were. They could be waiting up by the cars.

"See that girl over there?" Liliana pointed to Ava, who was sitting on a rock scrolling on her phone, the light reflecting off her glasses. "Go hang out with her for a little while. She's nice. Mostly."

The girls hesitated, one of them looking up at the path as if the guys might reappear. They did as they were told, though, and Liliana couldn't help but laugh at Ava's confused expression as she was crowded by the three sophomores. Ava met Liliana's eyes and Liliana gave her a goofy thumbs-up. Ava shot her an annoyed look but didn't send the girls away.

Liliana scanned the party, not really knowing who—

or what—she was looking for.

"Hey," Ruby said as she approached Liliana, a can of beer in each hand.

"Hey Ruby." Liliana shook her head distractedly at the beer Ruby offered her and continued watching the boys. Her throat was starting to feel worse, hot and swollen. Whatever was going to happen was going to happen soon. She could feel it.

She looked over at Ruby and realized with a jolt she'd forgotten about the most important boy at the party.

"Ruby, where's Diego?"

"Oh, he went off to pee on a cactus somewhere," Ruby said lightly, waving a hand toward the open desert.

Liliana looked in the direction Ruby gestured to, her skin prickling. Hot panic rippled up from her stomach into her chest and her eyes watered. The boy in her vision—the boy that was doomed to die tonight—was her own cousin. She felt sick as she realized the horrible truth.

I brought Diego here to die.

16

Liliana ran in the direction Ruby had gestured but slowed when she got too far from the firelight to see easily. She crept along through the cacti and scrub brush, calling out Diego's name. Her blood pounded through her, she could feel it in her chest, her throat, her mouth.

"Diego!" she called again, desperately searching in every direction for her lost cousin. He couldn't have gone that far into the desert. A silhouette appeared a few yards away and she sped up until she finally reached him. He had his back to her and was swaying as he peed onto some rocks.

"Diego! Come on, we have to go back, *now*."

Diego mumbled something over his shoulder and continued peeing, ignoring her.

"Diego, seriously, come on!" She was about to grab him, force him back to the party, when she heard it—a low hissing behind her.

She whipped around to face the creature, her body tense and screaming at her to run. Liliana forced herself to remain where she was, between her cousin and the monster. She eyed the rest of the party in the distance, a warm halo of light and laughter, close but not close enough.

She could barely see the monster in the faraway glow of the bonfire's light. It looked bigger than it had before, four grotesque human arms shot out on either side of the black-shelled body. A human torso encased in the same black shell with two giant, claw-like arms and a human head loomed over her. The creature's face was in shadow, but she could see the reflection on three pairs of eyes staring down at her.

Trembling, she backed up toward Diego, who was still blissfully unaware of what was right behind him.

"D-Diego ..." she murmured softly, "Diego you need to run. *Now*."

Diego zipped up his pants and slowly turned around.

"Okay, what—" Too late. Liliana froze as she saw the scorpion's tail, the tip dripping with silvery poison, waver a moment in the air before snapping down towards her.

Something hit her from the side–*hard*–and she was thrown out of the way of the scorpion's tail. She watched from the ground as the tail buried itself into Diego's chest instead.

"No!" she screamed, tears spilling down her face. Diego let out a small gasp and crumpled to the ground. *Too late, I was too late.*

The scorpion monster scuttled closer to Diego's body, its large pincers reaching for him.

"Leave him alone!" Liliana screamed as she threw the nearest rock at the monster. Its body whipped around to face her, and she immediately regretted drawing its attention. It lunged at her again, tail raised in striking position, when something dashed between her and the monster. In the darkness it was hard to make out, but it looked like a large coyote, except where there should have been fur there was just leathery skin. Long, sharp spikes grew along the creature's spine and its feet looked like those of an iguana, webbed with long hooked claws. It was turned away from her so she couldn't see its face, but she heard the deep, guttural growling sound it directed at the scorpion.

The scorpion's tail whipped down toward the creature, but it easily dodged, and the stinger hit nothing but dirt. The coyote-creature lunged at one of the hideous human arms holding the body up and sunk its teeth into its wrist. The scorpion made a high hissing sound and shook its arm vigorously, trying to release itself from the creature's jaws. Liliana backed up as much as she could, her eyes wide as she watched the two impossible beings attack each other. The scorpion grabbed the animal's body in one of its massive pincers and squeezed. The creature let out a sharp, pained yip as it twisted inside the scorpion's claw. The scorpion roared as the spikes on the animal's back stabbed through the black outer shell and into the meat of its pincer. Liliana winced as the scorpion's claw opened and the creature fell to the ground, landing with a thud on its side. The spikes that grew along its spine were covered in a steaming black liquid. The creature didn't move. Liliana took a step toward the injured animal, whatever it was.

A hand wrapped around her left arm and pulled—

hard. She went flying towards whoever had grabbed her and away from the scorpion and beast. Two strong arms wrapped around her body and lifted her easily off of the ground. The man threw her over his shoulder like she was nothing but a light jacket and then they moved, fast, away from the scorpion. Away from the coyote-lizard creature. Away from Diego.

"No!" she screamed, trying to release herself from the mystery man's grip. She pounded her fists against his back, wriggled as fiercely as she could to get him to let go, but he ignored her, moving further into the desert.

Finally, he set her down and she pulled away from him. She turned to run back to Diego but hesitated. It was pitch-black out and she could no longer see the glow of the bonfire. She couldn't see anything except for the dark outlines of towering saguaros all around her. The moon, a tiny sliver in the sky, provided barely any light.

She had no idea where she was.

She whipped around to face her captor. "*You*."

Mr. Reynard crossed his arms and looked at her as if she were being a petulant child—throwing a tantrum in a toy store. In the dark his amber eyes shone and she could just make out the deep red of his hair.

"Why did you do that? My cousin—"

"Is dead."

Liliana's mouth fell open and her stomach twisted painfully. She wrapped her arms around herself and looked out into the desert, searching for any indicator of where the party was, where Diego was.

"No, you don't know that." She saw the scorpion

sting him, but that didn't necessarily mean he was *dead*.

Mr. Reynard tipped his head to the side, studying her.

"*You* know, though. Don't you?" His voice was infuriatingly calm, but he was right.

She *did* know. It was a knowing that had settled inside of her, heavy and cold. She just didn't want to believe it. She tried so hard to stop it; she would have been able to stop it if—

"There was nothing you could have done," he said, crossing his arms. "He would have died regardless."

Liliana shook her head distractedly. She wanted to sit down but couldn't make her body move.

"It's all my fault. If I hadn't made Ruby come with me to the party, Diego wouldn't have come with her, and he never would have even been here!"

"He would have ended up here one way or another, that I can promise you."

"I should have been able to stop it, I could have—"

"No." He took a step toward her. "Once you've seen it, you can't stop it."

The words were uncomfortably familiar. Her abuela said the same thing earlier that day. She looked up into Mr. Reynard's glowing amber eyes and shivered.

"Come, you can't be out here any longer. I will take you home." He turned away from her and began walking away.

Home? She felt so completely worthless.

"No." Liliana refused to follow him. "Take me back to the party. Take me back to Diego."

Mr. Reynard stopped and turned to face her. He sighed and ran a hand through his autumn hair.

"I won't do that. The scorpion man and chupacabra are still out there, and I don't know how long they'll keep each other occupied."

Liliana stiffened. "You—you *know*?"

Mr. Reynard tilted his head as he considered her. "Know what?"

Liliana laughed—an ugly, broken sound that matched how she felt inside.

"Everything? You know *everything,* don't you?" She was losing it. She could feel herself cracking apart, but she needed answers. She needed to *know.* "What were those things? The scorpion man ... what is it? Why does it keep attacking me?" She choked down a sob. "Why is this happening to me?"

He stepped closer—*too* close. The scent of a forest fire wafted off of him, the same odd smell she had noticed in the classroom earlier that day. A mixture of fresh pine and smoke, a musk that didn't belong in the desert.

"The scorpion man ... is like you, in a way. Stronger, for now, but like you."

"Like me?" Her voice was barely a whisper.

He hesitated and backed away a few steps and looked up at the night sky.

"You are both legends—rather, descendants of legends."

Liliana thought of everything her abuela had told her about La Llorona and Faustina, her ancestors and the reason for her curse.

"He is a scorpion man, they are simple creatures, really. Strong, stupid, driven entirely by hunger. You, my dear, are something much more interesting. *You* are a banshee."

"*Banshee*?" She recognized the word, sort of. It brought to mind ugly, witchy women dressed all in black, wandering through villages screaming—*oh*. She raised a hand to her throat. She rubbed at her forehead, confusion bringing on an ache behind her eyes. Her abuela had told her she was cursed because of what her ancestor La Llorona had done ... now this man she didn't know was telling her she was a descendant of a banshee.

"*Banshee. Caoineag. Weeping Woman. Harbinger. Death's Messenger.* There have been lots of names for your kind, over the centuries." His eyes flicked over the top of her head, as if studying something deep in the darkness behind her. She fought the urge to turn and see what he was looking at and kept her eyes pinned on him.

"The world is changing," he continued when she didn't respond. "And you must be prepared. But now I must take you to safety—that scorpion man and chupacabra are still close, though the latter is likely dead by now and no longer a threat."

Liliana shook her head, her eyes tried to focus but she was feeling dizzy. She'd never heard of a scorpion man before, but she knew all about chupacabras. She grew up with the tales of the mysterious and deadly "goat suckers." Sometimes they were described as aliens, sometimes coyotes or dogs, sometimes reptiles or giant bats. What she saw somehow fit all of those descriptions, and yet none of them. But one thing was always the same—they were bloodsuckers. Killers.

A scream echoed out across the desert, the sound flowing over rock and weaving between cacti to reach Liliana's cold ears. She tensed and her stomach turned to stone.

Someone had found Diego.

17

The next morning, Liliana woke up with a headache and eyes that felt pinched. She slept fitfully, nightmares of scorpions and leather-skinned coyotes tormenting her all night. Everything that had happened after she heard that scream was a blur. She got home, but couldn't remember how or even falling asleep. She was still in her clothes from last night—torn and dirty.

Next to her on the bed her cell phone buzzed. Fifteen missed calls and too many texts to count. Everyone she knew showed up on her call list. Ava, Ruby, Jeremy, her mother, her father. Everyone ... except Diego.

Liliana sat on her bed, staring dumbly at the cell phone in her lap. It rang and she flinched, then pressed the mute button. Jeremy's name blinked at her. She couldn't muster the courage to answer.

She realized that Mr. Reynard must have brought her home, but everything that happened in the desert felt unreal. Her cousin was dead. She had seen him die, but some part of her still felt like if she didn't answer the calls, didn't hear the actual words, that maybe he was okay. Maybe all of it was just some crazy hallucination.

She didn't want to hear the words.

Liliana set the phone aside on the bed, face down, and drifted out of her room. A ghost of herself, she moved slowly down the hall to the kitchen. Ahead of her she could hear low voices and clattering dishes.

She lingered in the doorway to the kitchen for a moment and watched her little family. Her brother poked listlessly at some runny eggs on his plate, his eyes red. Her father had his arm wrapped around her mother and they were whispering things to each other by the sink. Liliana stepped forward into the room and immediately all eyes were on her.

"Liliana ..." her mother's voice broke, and she shook her head fiercely, tears squeezing from her eyes. Her dad left her mother in the kitchen and joined Liliana and Mateo in the small dining room.

"Liliana, were you at a party in the desert last night?"

She didn't know exactly what they knew. She had hoped it was less than this.

"Yes, for ... for a few minutes." She wasn't sure what to say. If she told them the truth, that she'd tried to save Diego and failed—so completely *failed*—what would they think of her? How would they look at her? She didn't read the texts or listened to the countless voicemails on her phone, clinging to the chance that everything was fine. Looking at her parents, at Mateo, she knew nothing would ever be fine again.

"Your friends were worried ... you didn't answer your phone. We all went out looking for you, after we heard ..." Her father's clear blue eyes studied Liliana. A question lingered in them that Liliana couldn't answer. *Wouldn't* answer. "You were asleep when we got back, in your bed. We ... we didn't want to wake you, but ... Liliana, last night Diego was attacked. Authorities think it was the same animal that killed that girl from your class—honey, he didn't—" her father's voice was blocked out by another voice, loud and deafening in her ears. A voice that sounded like a truck horn blaring and a metallic crunch, said *Ten years, three months, twelve days*.

"No," she choked out, tears dampening her cheeks.

"I know, it's awful," her father said gently, taking her into his arms. Pressing her wet face into the soft comfort of his sweatshirt, she shuddered as sobs took over her body. She cried for Diego. She cried for Isabel. She cried for her father, who she now knew would be dead in ten years, three months, twelve days. A car accident. She knew as clearly as she had known Diego's death.

Liliana pulled away slowly, her eyes falling on her mother and her brother. She could hear whispers of voices coming off of them like a cloying mist. Coming closer, growing louder.

"No," she repeated, her voice hoarse, her throat sore. She stepped away from her father, from her family, and ran back toward her room. She hesitated as she passed the bathroom and changed course, slipping inside and locking the door. People were a lot less likely to bother her in the bathroom than her bedroom.

She waited to see if someone would come after her, but no one did. She let out a relieved breath. Liliana didn't want to know when—and how—her mother and brother were going to die. She wished she hadn't listened to the voice floating around her father. She only had ten years left with him—it felt like a long time and yet no time at all.

Twenty-eight, she thought, a coldness spreading through her. *I'll be twenty-eight when my father dies. What will he miss? Liliana couldn't help but imagine her wedding without her father walking her down the aisle, her children growing up without their grandfather, her mother left alone.*

She turned away from the door and caught her reflection in the mirror. Her eyes were red and puffy from crying, dark half-moons shadowing them. Her hair was a tangled mess and dirt dusted her clothes. Filled with an overwhelming need to shower and wash the night off of her, she undressed, tearing her clothes off as if they were burning her. She gasped when she saw her naked body in the mirror.

Her whole right side was painted with black and blue bruises. She touched them gingerly and winced. She remembered hitting the ground hard when the chupacabra ran into her, but she had no idea she was so bruised. Didn't notice the pain blooming across one side of her body.

She took the hottest shower she could stand, scrubbing until her skin was raw. She closed her aching eyes, letting the hot water pour over her and enjoyed the momentary relief darkness gave her. That relief disappeared as images from the night before flashed in her mind—the scorpion monster, the chupacabra, Diego's body slumping to the ground. Mr. Reynard's flashing amber eyes.

Anger flooded through her—Mr. Reynard, if that

was even his real name, knew what was happening. He knew more about herself than she did, and he knew about the scorpion monster. She turned off the water—she needed to speak to Mr. Reynard. *Now.*

She dried off, then went to her bedroom to change. She threw on some shorts and a T-shirt and grabbed her phone. Her first period class was already half over, but that didn't matter.

She grabbed her bag and car keys and dashed through the house. She almost made it out the front door when her mother's voice stopped her.

"Liliana?"

She winced and turned to face her mother. She looked so ... old. Lines she'd never noticed before creased her mother's face and her cheeks sagged a little. "Where are you going? Mateo is staying home, we're all—you should stay home—your tía..."

Liliana shook her head. She didn't care what they thought of her. After last night nothing mattered anymore. Nothing except stopping that monster from killing again. She'd failed Diego last night, but she wouldn't let anyone else die.

She would find the monster and kill it—and there was only one person who could help her do it.

* * *

Liliana arrived at school and waited in her car until the bell signaling the end of first period rang. She watched as students moved like currents out of classrooms, into classrooms. She hurried to her English class—she didn't know if Mr. Reynard would be there, or how long he would be acting as substitute teacher.

Her heart pounded and her fingertips prickled with unease as she considered the possibility that he wasn't there. That he had left just as quickly as he came and she would never see him again. Never get any answers. *Please, please be there.*

She pushed against the flow of students coming out of the classroom and was flooded with relief when she saw him sitting behind the beaten-up desk. His amber eyes slid over to her and he waved away the girls that had accumulated around his desk.

"We need to talk—I need—I need *answers*. You have to *help me*," she begged, her voice low so the other students milling in or out of the classroom wouldn't hear her.

His eyes flicked quickly to something behind her, then focused on her again. "Not now," he said softly, a shadow of a purr in his tone. "I have a free period after this class, come back then and we'll talk."

Liliana looked around the filling classroom in a numb wonder—a wonder that anyone could go to class, teach a class, when the world was being ripped apart all around them. She didn't argue, though, only nodded and turned to leave. She nearly ran into Jeremy, who had been standing right behind her. He was unsmiling, his eyes suspicious. *How long had he been there? What had he heard?*

Jeremy opened his mouth to say something she already knew she didn't want to hear. Instead of waiting, she pushed past him and practically ran out of the building. Outside the sun glared down on her and she felt herself moving mechanically to her second period class. She didn't intend on going to class, but she didn't know what else to do.

When she sat down on her lab stool in her science class, whispers erupted from the other students surrounding her. They were the same whispers she'd heard yesterday about Isabel. Except this time they were about Diego— and about *her*. By now, she realized, they'd all heard some version of what happened last night. She had no idea what part she played in the stories making their way around school. Was she the victim who just lost her cousin? The villain who had disappeared from the party where her cousin was found dead? The sociopath who came to school as if she didn't even care about what happened? Even she wasn't sure what she was.

She eyed the empty stool across from her where Killian should be. The second bell rang and he still didn't appear. She was relieved more than anything; he was at the party last night. He saw her there. She didn't know what he knew, what else he might have seen, or heard. Even if he was as clueless as the rest of them were, she didn't want to talk to him. Didn't want to talk to *anyone*, really.

She sensed someone behind her and she turned to see Mr. Henderson looming. He had *that look*—a look he must have practiced over the years for just this situation.

"Liliana," he said softly. "I am so sorry for your loss. Let me know if you need anything." He gave her a soft pat on the shoulder.

She tried not to cry at that. She had tried to keep Diego's death at a distance in her mind. Liliana could see it, hear it, but she wouldn't allow herself to *feel* it.

She was afraid of what would happen if she did. Mr. Henderson's words made Diego's death more real. Now, forced to address what happened to him, she felt like she was breaking apart.

Her throat and eyes burned as she forced the tears back. She nodded, afraid if she opened her mouth to speak the sobs would come spilling out. He gave her a consoling smile that she found more annoying than comforting and made his way back to the front of the classroom. She glanced around the room—all eyes were on her. At the table next to hers Helsie stared at her with large, watery blue eyes while her lab partner Katie pretended to examine her nails, letting her lavender hair obscure her face. She preferred Katie's reaction.

Liliana pulled out a notebook and pen and turned her attention to the blank page in front of her. Mr. Henderson was lecturing at the front of the room, but she wasn't listening. She fidgeted on her uncomfortable stool and couldn't keep her eyes off the clock hanging on the wall above Mr. Henderson's head. All around her death whispers wafted off students like steam and Liliana tried to ignore them, but it was nearly impossible. She found if she didn't let herself focus on any single whisper, they stayed a nebulous mixture of sounds.

"Okay, now, if you'll pass these back." Mr. Henderson's real voice cut through the whispers. Liliana looked up and saw students passing back pieces of paper. She took hers and stared down at it. A quiz. *Great.*

"This is just a little pop quiz on what you all learned

about arachnids yesterday," Mr. Henderson said, eliciting a chorus of groans. Liliana stared down at the test and felt dizzy as she read the word *scorpion* over and over. She took better notes than she usually did yesterday about scorpions, and somewhere in her mind she knew the answers to every question. But the words blurred together, and she couldn't force herself to care about the quiz.

When the bell rang Liliana crumpled the test into a ball and threw it in her bag.

She was the first one out of the classroom, eager to get back to Mr. Reynard. She passed the large black willow, its tendrils swaying back and forth like jellyfish tentacles. She watched the waving branches as she walked by, mesmerized by the motion. Someone stepped in front of her and she fell into the person, causing him to stumble. She regained her balance and winced when she saw who she'd bumped into.

Ben's eyes were red-rimmed and puffy, his shoulder-length, light-brown hair greasy and tangled. There was a hollowness to his face—he looked like he hadn't eaten or slept in days.

"Liliana," he said, his voice hoarse. "I am so sorry—so sorry to hear about Diego." He sounded like he was on the verge of tears; she'd never seen someone so destroyed before. She never told him she was sorry about what happened to Isabel. She didn't know him. But now they had something in common—they'd both lost people they loved to the same monster.

"Thank you," she forced out. "Isabel ... it's so ..." she trailed off as Ben's eyes became watery. *Oh no he's going to cry*. She didn't have time for this. She needed to get to Mr. Reynard. "Um, I—I have to go," she said lamely. Ben nodded and rubbed the back of his hand against his wet eyes. "I'll, um, let's talk ... later."

She wasn't sure Ben had heard her. He was already drifting away, and in a blink, he was gone. She took a deep breath and let it out. She needed to avoid any more run-ins.

Liliana decided to go around the outside of the school to the English classroom instead of through the crowded quad. She needed to avoid running into any of her friends, or worse, *Jeremy*. She remembered how he had looked at her earlier, his blue eyes had been dark, stormy, and his mouth a tense, straight line. Liliana didn't returned any of his calls. She went to that party without telling him. He was mad, and he had every right to be. She just didn't have the time or energy to deal with that right now.

She almost made it to the classroom without running into anyone else. Almost.

Becca was leaning up against the wall next to the door Liliana had to go through. She was using her phone as a makeshift mirror as she reapplied her peony-pink lipstick. Liliana hesitated, uncertain if she should breeze past her or hide until she left. Before she could decide, Becca's eyes shifted from her own reflection and landed on Liliana.

Mierda. Here we go.

A strange look crossed Becca's face when she saw Liliana standing there. Her cheeks were flushed and she looked quickly around as if Liliana might have some gang waiting to jump her. Becca stuffed her lipstick and phone into her bag and shot Liliana her standard glare as she passed.

Liliana turned to watch her go, suspicion tingling at the back of her neck. Becca seemed startled, as if Liliana had caught her doing something she shouldn't be. But what?

Liliana turned toward the door to her English class and shoved Becca out of her mind. Becca was nothing, was inconsequential.

She pushed open the door to the classroom and let out a breath of relief when she saw that it was empty, aside from Mr. Reynard sitting at the teacher's desk. Part of her was afraid he wouldn't be there—that he disappeared back to wherever he came from to avoid dealing with her.

He leaned back in his chair, watching her with his sly, calculating eyes.

"Well? What can I do for you?"

For a second she faltered. Was this really the same man who had saved her from the scorpion monster the night before? Hundreds of questions clamored over each other in her mind, and she paused, speechless for a moment, not knowing where to start.

"Who are you?" was the first one to slip out.

He nodded to himself, as if he knew this was what she would ask first and that he was a little disappointed she'd been so predictable. She glared down at him and crossed her arms, waiting.

"Come closer," he said, gesturing. He leaned forward, the wooden chair creaking as it settled back into its usual position. He rested his arms on the paper-littered desk in front of him. Liliana hesitated, annoyed by this man who seemed to enjoy playing with her. She took a few steps closer.

"Now, listen."

She stood there for a second. Two.

"I don't hear anything."

"Yes." He looked at her as if all should be clear now.

"I—I don't understand," she admitted sourly.

He sighed. "You don't hear the voices."

Liliana blinked, then realized what he had said was true. The death whispers had become almost natural to her, a buzz in the background of everything. But here, with him, she heard nothing.

"What does that mean?"

He closed his eyes tightly, as if she had irritated him so much with her slowness that he needed to pull himself together before answering.

"You don't hear anything," he said slowly, "because Death is not waiting for me."

Liliana couldn't help but raise her eyebrows at that.

"You hear voices telling you when people will die and you've been attacked by a scorpion man, but *this* you find hard to believe?"

She shrugged. "Fine, let's say that's true—you're never going to die. Why? What are you, exactly?" Liliana eyed his long limbs and dark-red hair, his laughing amber eyes. She inhaled his strange forest fire scent.

"I've been many things, had many names, over the centuries. Kitsune, Huxian, the Nine-Tailed Fox, Cadmean Vixen ... but at the beginning, I was the

Teumessian fox." He smiled coyly, as if he expected her to be impressed. She wasn't.

"The what now?"

He frowned. "Really? The Teumessian fox? Created by the gods, destined to never be captured...?"

Liliana stared at him blankly.

"Well, that's disappointing." He shook his head as he rose from his chair. Liliana tilted her head up to look at him as he towered over her. Teumessian fox. She thought of the eyes watching her from within the black willow's branches, the fox that saved her from the scorpion man the first time.

"You're ... you're the fox. But—how?" Her head started to hurt as she tried to put it all together. This man—this *substitute teacher*—was also a ... fox?

"Who I am doesn't really matter," he said lightly with a wave of his hand. "What matters right now is who the *scorpion man* is."

Liliana recoiled, disgusted and surprised, at how casually he mentioned the creature that murdered her cousin less than twenty-four hours ago.

"He's here, at this school somewhere. Trying to pretend that everything is normal. He might not even know what he is. We need to find him when he's in his *human* form. He's too powerful to take on when he's changed, as you've seen."

Liliana felt the blood rush out of her face and her hands curled into tight fists at her sides. "That ... that *thing* ... is a person? Someone I *know*?"

"Most likely."

Liliana took a dizzy step backward and slumped into

a nearby desk chair. She thought of the hundreds of students in the school.

"How—how do we find him? How do we figure out who it is?"

"Well, he'll be your age—eighteen."

Liliana blinked at that.

"Eighteen? How do you know?"

Mr. Reynard took a deep breath and looked around the empty classroom as if he was searching for a model to show her. Or a map.

"You came into your powers on your eighteenth birthday, correct? Well, it's the same for him. Don't ask me why, I don't know." He waved a hand at her and she swallowed the question she was about to ask. "So. Since the killings have started recently, his birthday must be recent."

He walked back over to his desk and picked up a piece of paper and handed it to her. A list of names with birthdays by each one stared back at her.

"I pulled those from the school's system. It's every boy in school who is eighteen. Focus on the ones at the top of the list, they have the most recent birthdays."

Liliana looked down at the first name on the list: Killian Davies.

"This one." She pointed to Killian's name on the paper. "He's always acting weird, always angry, and he was at the party last night. He wasn't in class today."

Mr. Reynard nodded. "Good, start with him."

"What do you mean *start with him*? Aren't *you* going to do something?"

He ran his fingers through his deep-red hair and

slumped back down in the teacher's chair.

"I *am* doing something," he replied as he typed something into his computer, then scribbled something onto a yellow sticky note. He peeled it off the stack and offered it to her.

She took the note and saw that he had written an address on it.

"That's Killian's address," he explained, a touch of exasperation in his voice. "If he's not at school today, try his house."

Liliana blinked at the address. The last thing she wanted to do was go to Killian's house.

"By myself? You're not coming?"

"I have more important things to attend to. I'm sure you can handle it. It's just a boy." He shrugged. "For now. He'll be in his human form until sunset. After that ..."

He didn't need to finish his sentence; Liliana knew all too well what would happen after sunset. She tried to swallow but her throat was sore again, swollen and tight.

"It won't be easy—focus on the names on the list, but keep a close eye on everyone around you—who is acting differently, whose friends seem concerned."

She nodded, more to herself than to him. She turned to leave, then paused.

"What about that other creature—the chupacabra?"

Mr. Reynard shrugged. "I searched for it," he admitted, "but I didn't find any sign of the chupacabra aside from some blood on the ground. The scorpion man most likely ate it."

Liliana felt sick. "*Ate* it?"

"Why do you think he's been attacking people? For amusement? No, he is hungry. Every time he makes a kill, it seems that something interrupts him. The girl—she was mostly intact when they found her. Your cousin—well that was a foolish choice on the scorpion man's part. So many people around. He keeps killing—but never gets to eat."

"That's disgusting," Liliana murmured, her hands holding her stomach. She was on the cusp of vomiting and looked around the room for something to puke into.

Mr. Reynard shrugged.

"Everything has to eat."

18

Liliana let the tide of students pull her through the school. She didn't feel like one of them anymore. They were water and she was just floating debris.

She watched them moving around her, bewildered they could just go about their day as if nothing at all was different. As if two of their classmates weren't recently murdered. She searched the faces of the boys she passed, wondering if any of them was the scorpion man. They all seemed so normal. It *had* to be Killian.

Liliana separated from the stream of people heading to the cafeteria and instead turned toward the parking lot. Someone grabbed her arm and she jumped, whipping around to see who it was.

Ava was standing behind her, her expression serious. She let go of Liliana's arm.

"What happened to you last night?" She stared at Liliana through her black-framed glasses, her mouth a soft frown. "We all tried to call you—you disappeared and then ... and then ... Lil, I thought you were ..."

Liliana stiffened as tears spilled down her friend's face. Ava removed her glasses and wiped angrily at the tears wetting her cheeks.

Liliana didn't know what to do. If she should be comforting, explaining, or crying herself. She wanted to do all three but felt like she'd suddenly been turned to stone.

She wished Ruby was there. If anyone would believe Liliana's crazy story, it was Ruby. She felt a pang of guilt—Ruby loved Diego. She was there when ... maybe was the one to find ... Liliana swallowed painfully. She didn't return any of Ruby's calls or texts, either. Didn't reach out to see if she was okay. She just ... wasn't ready to face her.

"You can tell me," Ava said softly, "what happened last night? Where did you go?"

She wanted to trust Ava and tell her everything. She wanted desperately not to feel so alone in all of this. But she knew she couldn't—it was all too much to believe.

"I—I don't really want to talk about it," Liliana replied, not untruthfully.

Ava looked hurt but nodded. "I understand," she said. "Do you—do you want to go home? Or to my house? You shouldn't be here today."

Liliana *did* want to go home, but she couldn't. She glanced at the paper with all the suspects' names Mr. Reynard gave her. She needed to go to Killian's house. She shoved the piece of paper into her bag.

"I'm sorry, I gotta go." She turned, rushing towards the parking lot. Behind her, Ava called her name, but Liliana didn't look back.

* * *

Liliana stopped her car in front of a run-down two-story bungalow. The blue paint, washed out from years in the Arizona sun, peeled off in strips and the wood around the windows was cracked. A car that might have been impressive sixty years ago was missing its wheels and resting on cement blocks in the driveway. The yard was just dirt and weeds.

Liliana didn't want to go up to that house. Even if she didn't suspect Killian of being a murderous scorpion man she wouldn't want to go up to that house.

"That's the sort of house you don't come back out of," she muttered to herself.

As she stared up at the run-down building, she felt for her powers, searched them out inside of her, but felt nothing. With no one nearby she didn't even hear any death whispers. She envied the scorpion man at that moment. They both woke up on their eighteenth birthdays with powers: but hers were *useless* while his were dangerous. She wanted to feel strong, a force to be reckoned with. Instead, she hid in her car, afraid to approach a house that may be home to a monster—or just a surly teenage boy.

She leaned forward and looked out the windshield at the sky. The sun was high, dusk hours away. If Killian was the scorpion man, she had plenty of time left before he transformed. She should be safe—for now.

She forced herself to get out of the car and walk up to the broken-down house. *This is the part of the movie where I would yell at the dumb ass about to traipse right into certain danger. Now look at me—I'm the dumb ass.*

She made her way carefully up the dilapidated wooden steps leading to the front door. Old beer bottles filled with drowned cigarette butts littered the porch and a pile of ratty shoes sat outside the front door.

The screen door's wire mesh was ripped in places and the metal at the bottom was bent inward, as if someone had kicked it in.

She gingerly pulled the screen door open and knocked, hard and quick, before she lost what sliver of nerve she had.

Liliana let the screen door smack shut and took a few steps back. She thought about the scorpion man—the creature that had attacked her twice now. The face with too many pairs of eyes, the hard black shell instead of skin. She prayed that Mr. Reynard was right, that he would be human until dusk.

As the door eased opened she realized she didn't have a plan. Panic rushed through her—Mr. Reynard had given her Killian's address, but not a *plan. What am I supposed to do with him?*

She studied the man who opened the door. It wasn't Killian, but there was enough similarity in appearance that she guessed this was an older brother. The man was tall and thinner than Killian, his missing shirt revealing a concave chest and visible ribs underneath his pale skin. He had a can of beer in one hand and a glazed look in his eyes that told her it wasn't the first one of the day.

"What?" The man's voice was hoarse and low, hearing it made her own throat hurt more. His death whisper wafted off of him toward her and she let it come. It was a long, quiet sigh and nothing more.

Six months, one week, three days.

Liliana grimaced at how soon his death was, but she wasn't particularly surprised. He looked half-dead already. He raised the beer to his lips, and she saw that the inside of his arm was covered in bruises and riddled with small, scabby puncture wounds.

"Um, is, uh—is Killian here?"

The man grinned showing a mouth full of crooked teeth in varying shades of yellow. He turned his head and called out into the dark house.

"Killian! You have a *sen-yo-reeta* here for you!" He opened the screen door, pushing it out toward her and gesturing for her to come inside. Everything inside of her screamed not to.

She swallowed, wishing again that she was cursed with a power other than knowing when people would die. Something like fire balls, or mind control, or ... really *anything* else.

"My friend is waiting," she blurted and gestured toward her parked car. She hoped he couldn't see that there wasn't actually anyone in the car. He smirked and rolled his eyes.

"Sweetheart, you're not my type."

Liliana felt like she might throw up, right there on the pile of shoes by the door. But she held it together and walked quickly past him, trying to make herself as small as possible to avoid brushing his arm as she passed.

She flinched as the screen door slammed shut behind her. Inside the house was dark, the only light coming in through streaks on the dirty windows. She nearly choked on the stale, cigarette-smoke air and desperately wanted to open a window. Stained cardboard boxes leaned against the walls, piled on top of each other in stacks that almost reached the ceiling. Paint was peeling off the walls to reveal a black mold growing underneath and there were large, yellow stains on the ceiling. Dirty clothes and trash, mostly fast-food wrappers and empty beer cans, were strewn around on the floor. Her eyes were wide as she took it all in, then caught Killian's brother watching her. She tried to relax her face, to look unsurprised, unbothered. He gestured at the stairs.

"He's up there."

Killian's brother disappeared down the hall and into one of the rooms. She hesitated, no part of her wanted to go up those stairs. She wasn't even sure they would hold her weight.

A dark figure appeared at the top of the staircase—Killian, in his usual black sweatshirt and ripped jeans. His arms were wrapped tightly around himself and he looked paler than normal. His dyed-black hair looked greasy, as if he hadn't showered in weeks.

"What are you doing here?" he rasped as he stared daggers at her.

She took a step closer and listened. The death whisper floating around him sounded like the wind. *Four months, one week, two days.*

Liliana's eyes widened as she listened to Killian's death. He was going to die *soon*—only a couple months before his brother. That didn't really tell her anything useful, though, at least nothing related to him being the scorpion man.

"Get out!" Killian yelled. Liliana realized that she was, once again, staring at him without replying.

"Killian, sorry, I just—um—wanted to make sure you're ... okay."

It was a lame excuse but the best she could come up with. He narrowed his eyes at her and scoffed.

"Sure, like you give a shit about me. Perfect little Liliana with her perfect little life—do you get a kick out of seeing this?" Killian gestured around at the run-down house, the trash on the floor. "You going to go back to school and tell everyone what a shithole I live in?"

Liliana felt a pang in her chest at his words. *Is that really what he thinks of me?*

She looked away from him, her stomach twisting as she realized he was right. If she'd seen this last week, before everything changed ... she wouldn't have told *everyone*, but probably would have told her friends.

She caught her reflection in a dirty, cracked mirror that hung on the wall by the bottom of the stairs. Liliana stared at her smooth, brown face, unmarred by the teenage acne most people she knew struggled with, her long, wavy dark hair, and her arresting brown eyes. She was pretty, but she never thought she was vain about it. Her beauty never really felt like her own, anyway. It was a gift passed to her from her mother; she couldn't take credit for it.

She turned away from the mirror as she heard Killian take a few steps down the stairs toward her. She could see him better now that he was closer. Liliana squinted at him, at the odd shadow around him, one that didn't lie the way it should. She took a step onto the stairs toward him, gawking at the shadow swirling around Killian's neck like a scarf of dark smoke.

"What ..." She took another step closer and felt the

anger, the hatred, pouring off of him. The shadow went still, and a pair of pure-black eyes blinked out of the smoky darkness.

"Mine," a cold, slithering voice hissed. "Death may not have him, not yet."

Liliana stumbled backward and nearly fell off the stairs. She grabbed onto the railing to steady herself.

"I—I don't *want* him," she hissed back at the shadow creature.

"What?" Killian snapped.

"What *do* you want?" The shadow purred as it poured over Killian's shoulder, then twisted itself around to wrap its shadow-body back around his neck. A wispy tendril of shadow reached up and stroked Killian's face. Liliana's stomach churned.

"I want—" Liliana panicked. She didn't know what she wanted and couldn't remember why she was there. She closed her eyes tightly, breaking eye contact with the shadow snake. Her head cleared. "I want to know if he's the scorpion man."

"The *what*?" Killian yelled as he stormed down the stairs toward her. She was forced backward and her back hit the front door. "Get out! Get out! Get out!" he shrieked in her face. The rotten-meat stench of his breath nearly made her gag.

The shadow slithering around his neck echoed Killian in its cold, damp voice.

"Get out, get out, get out," it sang, unbearably amused.

Her shaking hand fumbled for the doorknob behind her. She kept her eyes firmly on the dark shadow around

Killian's neck and struggled to get the door open.

"Tell me," she pleaded as she clumsily opened the door inward, forcing Killian to step a few feet back. She could feel the sun on her back and smell the fresh air outside. She wanted nothing more than to turn and run and never look back. But she had to know.

"Tell me!" she yelled. "Tell me and I'll leave!"

Killian's pale face bloomed red and his mouth twisted into a sneer. "I don't know what you're talking about!" he yelled back. "Get out of my house you crazy bitch!"

The shadow around Killian's neck let out an amused sigh.

"No, little banshee," the shadow murmured, "he is not what you seek."

19

Liliana slammed her car door and quickly pushed the automatic lock button. Her hands were shaking and she gripped the steering wheel to quiet them. She wasn't sure what she was more afraid of—Killian or the shadow snake wrapped around his neck that *spoke* to her.

She believed the shadow when it told her that Killian wasn't the scorpion man, but the shadow itself just raised more questions. Questions she hoped Mr. Reynard would be able to answer later.

Liliana picked up the sheet of paper he gave her and looked down the list again, at the names directly after Killian's. Julio Varga, Ben Thompson, Finn Collins ... Jeremy Becker. Liliana stared at her boyfriend's name as the blood drained from her face. She remembered Jeremy's birthday, of course. It'd been a month ago—he had a big party at his house.

No, she thought, shaking her head. *It can't be him.* But something inside of her prickled at the possibility. She looked back at the first name after Killian's—Julio Varga. Julio and Diego used to be best friends, before Ruby. They'd both fallen for her and they'd both refused to back off. Ruby had pretended the whole thing was annoying but Liliana knew she had loved every second of it.

Liliana smiled softly to herself, remembering the ludicrous lengths Diego went to impress Ruby. He left flowers on her doorstep every morning, climbed on top of the cafeteria building just to get her attention. It paid off—she'd picked him over Julio in the end. Liliana's smile faded as she remembered Diego was dead. She'd let herself forget, just for a second. She'd tried not to think about him, tried to keep the sadness away, but here it was in full force. She let go and let herself cry in her car for a few minutes, hidden from everyone she knew, before she forced herself to stop. Strands of her long hair stuck to her damp face and she pushed them away. Liliana blinked away the last of her tears and took a few deep breaths. She could mourn her cousin properly *after* she caught his killer.

The piece of paper in her lap was now splattered with tears, but the first few names were still clear. It was hard for her to imagine Julio as a monster. He and Diego weren't friends anymore but they weren't enemies, either. Diego had a connection to Isabel, too, though not a strong one. They dated briefly freshman year, but it wasn't serious.

Her eyes slid to the name after Julio's—Ben Thompson. Ben was devastated after Isabel's death and was still a complete mess. It was hard for her to imagine Ben hurting Isabel, and she was pretty sure he had no connection to Diego.

Then there was Finn Collins. Pumpkin-haired first

baseman of the varsity baseball team and Helsie's on-again-off-again boyfriend. He and Diego had been on the baseball team together, but she didn't think he knew Isabel.

Julio was the only one that had a connection to both Diego and Isabel. He was in her last class of the day; she would try him next.

The end-of-lunch bell rang just as she was pulling her car into the parking lot. She grabbed her bag, shoving the list of names inside, and dashed to her next class. Calculus dragged by and Liliana struggled to pay attention to the teacher's droning about hyperbolic angles. Liliana knew all this stuff already, anyway.

When the bell rang, she raced to her next class, US Government, where she hoped to see Julio. She didn't know if he came to school today, and she really hoped she wouldn't have to make another home visit.

She slid into her seat and watched impatiently as students drifted into the classroom. Finally, Julio strolled in, his thick, dark hair perfectly styled, flashing a contagious smile. Liliana couldn't help but smile back, even though he wasn't really smiling at her. It was impossible not to be captivated by Julio; he drew people to him without trying. He exuded a natural charm few could resist. She'd never admitted it to Diego or Ruby, but she'd always been surprised Ruby had chosen her cousin over Julio.

Liliana kept an eye on him and the clock, her fingers tapping impatiently against her desk. When the bell rang she leapt out of her seat and caught up to Julio as he left the classroom. She grabbed him gently by the arm and he turned, his expression softening when he saw her.

"Liliana," Julio said, a warm sadness in his tone. "I am so sorry about Diego. I know we ... grew apart ... but I'll still miss him."

A strong stench of baby powder and roses wafted over her as Becca approached them, an ugly smile twisting her mouth.

Oh, God, what now?

Becca's eyes flicked to look past Liliana at something behind her, then quickly refocused on Liliana. "I just wanted to ask Julio," Becca slid an arm through Julio's as a saccharine smile slid across her face, "if he could give me a ride home today?" Her tone was so sickly sweet it made Liliana physically ill. Becca didn't take her eyes off Liliana as Julio looked back and forth between the two girls, confusion darkening his usually bright expression.

"Uh, sure, but you're not really on my—"

"Thank you so much!" Becca interrupted. "Let's go, I'm sure you're done with that." Becca waved her hand at Liliana as if she were some stray dog Julio had paused to pet. Liliana once again found herself wishing that she had fire ball powers. Liliana smirked—she might not be able to throw fireballs, but she *could* know how much longer Becca had on this earth. She focused on the death whisper wafting off Becca. It was difficult to separate hers from the countless others all around her, but there it was, a voice that sounded like a dripping faucet.

Sixty-two years, six months, four days.

Liliana didn't love how disappointed she was to hear the long life Becca had ahead of her. And she had no idea what a dripping faucet meant. Before she could object, Becca pulled Julio away toward the parking lot, and Liliana was left alone and frozen with indecision. She considered going after them, but couldn't think of anything to say once she caught up. Julio didn't have a shadow snake monster wrapped around him to tell her what she needed to know. She had no idea how she was going to find out if he was the scorpion man or not. He didn't *seem* like a monster, but ...

"There you are," a firm, but familiar, voice said into her ear. She spun around to see Jeremy, his face tight and his icy-blue eyes flashing. "Why were you talking to *Julio*?"

Liliana's heart thudded too quickly inside her chest. She opened her mouth to speak but no sound came out. His hand gripped her arm a little too hard as he pulled her close to him. She looked up at him, surprised.

"I know you must be sad, because of what happened to Diego," he said tersely into her ear. "But you will explain to me what you were doing at that party in the first place."

Panic raced through her; she had no idea what to tell Jeremy.

"I—"

"I asked her to go with me."

Liliana turned to see Ava standing a few feet away, her hands on her hips and her eyes sharply glaring at Jeremy over her glasses. Liliana felt Jeremy release her arm and she took a wobbly step back from him.

"Ava," Jeremy said, a practiced smile slipping across his face. "That's interesting, I thought you hated parties?"

Liliana rubbed at her arm and glanced nervously at Ava.

Ava shrugged at Jeremy. "I wanted to go to that one." She stared him down, daring him to challenge her.

Jeremy made a sound in his throat that Liliana couldn't decipher. He didn't seem to believe Ava but didn't have any proof that she was lying. He turned to look at Liliana and she tensed.

"We'll talk later," he said quietly. He shot Ava a glare before following Julio and Becca toward the parking lot. Liliana hoped he was just going to his car and not going after Julio. The thought surprised her, Jeremy would never hurt Julio—he would never hurt anyone. Would he?

Liliana turned her gaze from Jeremy's retreating back to meet Ava's worried eyes.

"Are you—okay?" she asked.

"Honestly I don't even know," Liliana replied, wrapping her arms around herself as if she were cold despite the oven-level heat outside. "I get why he's mad—I've been avoiding him, and I didn't tell him I was going to that party, and then—"

"*¡Basta!*" Ava stepped close to Liliana, her face only a few inches from her own. "Don't do that. He doesn't own you. You don't have to ask him for permission to do things." Ava paused as she studied Liliana's face. "Or for forgiveness just for existing."

Liliana avoided her eyes, her face warming under Ava's scrutiny. She knew what Ava saw, how it must have looked. But it wasn't that simple; no one is perfect but Jeremy comes pretty close. Liliana thought of the birthday party he'd thrown for her, all the times he'd been there for her. He always protected her.

"Things are just so crazy right now," Liliana replied, stepping back from Ava. She lost her chance with Julio, and for all she knew, she just let a murdering scorpion monster take Becca home.

"Liliana, I really need to talk to you, like *really* talk. Can we go somewhere, my house?"

Liliana found herself shaking her head no. She didn't have time to go with Ava. She missed her chance with Julio and still needed to talk to Ben and Finn. She had no idea where Ben was, but she had a pretty good idea where she could find Finn.

"Later, Ava, really—I just can't right now."

Her throat throbbed, tightening. She didn't have much time left to stop the next death.

"I'll call you later, okay?" Liliana said, forcing a smile. "I promise."

Ava opened her mouth to say something but Liliana turned and jogged away, leaving her friend standing alone for the second time, a broken look on her face.

20

Liliana let her fingers curl into the holes of the chain link fence protecting the bleachers from the flying baseballs. The team practiced throwing drills, the ball whipping from the catcher to third, third to second, second to first, first to pitcher, pitcher to catcher, and all over again. Liliana was only interested in the first baseman, though—his telltale pumpkin-orange hair pushing out from underneath a sweat-stained baseball cap. She tried not to look at shortstop—some scrawny junior she didn't know in Diego's position. He hadn't even been dead for twenty-four hours and they had already replaced him. Going ahead with practice as if nothing had happened.

"Hey girl, heeey," Helsie drawled in her sticky-sweet southern accent as she bounced over to Liliana, her blonde curls pulled into an equally bouncy ponytail. Liliana couldn't help but cringe.

"Hi, Helsie," Liliana mumbled in return.

"Whatcha doin' here?" Helsie asked. "These practices are *so* boring."

Liliana struggled to think of some excuse, but Helsie cut her off before she could reply.

"Oh. My. God. I am so sorry!" Helsie half-screamed, her hand flying to cover her mouth. "I forgot, Diego was on the team and—you must be—I am *so sorry!*"

Liliana wished Helsie would shut up and go away. She didn't respond, hoping her silence would be hint enough. Then she realized—Helsie was there for Finn, too. Liliana squeezed her eyes tightly together in irritation. Of course. Why wouldn't his girlfriend watch him practice?

Liliana was about to scream in frustration when Mr. Reynard's words floated through her head.

"Keep a close eye on everyone around you—who is acting differently, whose friends seem concerned."

If anyone knew if something was different about Finn, it'd be Helsie. She forced the irritation from her expression as best she could and turned to the bubbly girl next to her.

"You know, I really just need someone to talk to right now," she said as pathetically as she could. Helsie's bright-blue eyes went wide and she nodded furiously, a couple of loose curls bounced around her face.

"Whatever you need, girl," Helsie said as she grabbed Liliana's arm and led her to a shady spot on the bleachers.

Helsie sat down on the worn wood bench and practically pulled Liliana down next to her. She hooked her arm with Liliana's and tugged her closer. Liliana forced herself not to pull away.

"You poor thing," Helsie cooed as she hugged Liliana's arm. "Diego was your ... cousin, right?"

The last thing she wanted to talk about was Diego.

Her throat was hot and swollen and she wasn't sure it was entirely her death power doing it. She couldn't cry again, not here, not in front of Helsie.

"You know, I don't think I can talk about him right now. It's too upsetting." Liliana hated herself. She *was* upset about Diego's death, but it still all felt like an act. Using Diego's death to get information felt wrong, and her stomach twisted.

"Why don't you talk instead," Liliana tried, forcing the guilt away. "How's things going with Finn?" Liliana nodded in the general direction of the field where Finn was tossing and catching baseballs.

"Oh, just fine," Helsie said, finally releasing Liliana's arm. "He's been real sad about Diego."

Watching Finn happily throwing the ball back and forth to his teammates made Liliana doubt that, but she just nodded.

"What about Isabel?" Liliana asked as casually as possible. "Did he know her?"

"Mm, I don't know, he might have had a class with her, not sure. They weren't friends or anything."

Liliana nodded again. That didn't surprise her; Isabel didn't really run in the same circles as Finn. She struggled to think of other questions to ask Helsie, questions more discreet than *has Finn turned into a murderous scorpion monster lately?*

Liliana jumped as the coach blew his high-pitched whistle. She and Helsie watched as the boys ran off the field and into the dugout.

"Coach will give them one of his little speeches," Helsie explained, "then they'll be released. Usually only takes a few minutes."

Liliana felt deflated. She'd failed to learn anything about Julio, and she had a feeling she was about to fail with Finn as well. She didn't know what she was doing—she wasn't a detective and didn't know what to ask, if there was anything she *could* ask.

Her sore throat was getting worse—she was running out of time and still had no idea who the scorpion man was. She tensed as she remembered the monster's tail striking at her last night. How *she'd* almost been the dead person everyone was quickly moving on from. *If I had never gone to that party ... the party!*

She wanted to kick herself for being so dense. She saw Helsie and Finn at the party, just before she was attacked by the scorpion man. She glanced down at the field to see the players dispersing from the dugout, Finn heading straight to her and Helsie. She didn't have much time.

"Last night," she asked hurriedly, before Finn reached them, "did Finn ever leave you alone? Even for just a minute?"

Helsie wrapped a long blonde curl around her perfectly manicured finger as she considered. "No— well, yes, but—" Helsie paused and looked at Liliana as if to say, *are you sure you want to hear this?*

"Go on."

"He left me alone when—well, when Ruby found Diego. He ran over to help ..."

Liliana winced and closed her eyes tightly against the tears that were threatening to fall. *Ruby* had found Diego. Liliana heard the scream when Diego was found—it was the last thing she heard before she woke up in her bedroom hours later. *That had been Ruby screaming.*

Liliana opened her eyes to see that Finn was just a few yards away now, and she didn't want to get sucked into some awkward conversation with him. She wasn't sure she could handle any more condolences.

"Thanks!" Liliana called behind her to Helsie as she took off at a jog, away from the baseball field and toward the parking lot. If Finn had never left Helsie's side, he couldn't be the scorpion man. She was able to cross one more name off her list.

Liliana was almost to the parking lot when she felt someone watching her. She stopped and turned, her eyes scanning the grounds until they stopped on Mr. Reynard. He stepped out of the shadow of a building and sauntered over to her, as if he didn't have a single care in the world. As if monsters weren't roaming around murdering people.

He wasn't wearing his tweed blazer anymore, and he'd pushed the sleeves up on the white dress shirt he was wearing. His hair shone like copper in the sun.

"Well? Any progress?"

Something about this little check-in irritated her. She was doing all the work, and he was just going to what— stroll up and collect her intel? Then what? She eyed the man suspiciously, he'd done nothing but help her, and yet something inside her told her not to trust him. She realized she was clenching her teeth and made herself relax her jaw. She had no choice—she had to tell him what she'd learned about Killian and Finn. She gave him an abridged version of events, then described the shadowy entity wrapped around Killian.

"Do you know what that is?" she urged when he didn't respond.

Mr. Reynard nodded absently as he gazed off into the distance, lost in thought. "Just a shade."

"A shade? What's that?"

"It's actually sort of amusing," he said with a feline smile. "They latch onto someone and suck all the joy out of them until they are nothing but anger and sadness."

Liliana's mouth fell open. "What is amusing about *that*?"

"Oh, that's not the funny part. Historically ... well." He chuckled. "Historically, shades are sworn to serve death, sworn to serve *you*."

"I am *not* death!" she screeched. A few boys leaving baseball practice shot her startled looks as they passed by to go to their cars.

"No, of course not. But you're ... death-adjacent. Imagine there's a death food chain, and you are here—" he raised a hand in the air, "and shades are here." He lowered his hand a considerable distance. "You're just new, that's all. You'll learn."

"I don't *want* to learn! I just want all of this to *stop*!"

He shrugged, a bored expression on his face. He looked past her as if he was done talking to her and might wander off without another word.

"Okay, so, if I wanted—I could make the shade leave Killian alone?" she asked, a little embarrassed. Mr. Reynard's eyes moved back to her.

"Yes, but it'd just find someone else. Is there someone else you'd like to give to the shade?"

Liliana thought about that. Becca came to mind, but only because she'd so recently irritated her. Becca was truly awful, but mostly harmless. The thought of intentionally siccing the shade on her—on anyone—made her squeamish.

"When is this boy destined to die?"

Liliana blinked. The question took her off guard, but she tried to remember what Killian's death whisper had said. "I don't remember," she admitted. "But it was soon, a few months, I think."

"Ah, what's the point, then? Let the shade have him."

"Let ..." Liliana couldn't believe Mr. Reynard could be so callous, so cavalier, about a person's life. Sure, Killian wasn't her favorite person, but the idea of him living the remainder of his life that way, so angry ... and then to die so young ...

Liliana looked down at the ground and watched as a line of red ants marched past.

"If it's any consolation, Killian's anger, his hatred, the shade didn't make him that way. Just ... increased what was already there."

Liliana considered this, but it didn't lessen the guilt that wrapped tightly around her internal organs. No one was born angry. Someone made him that way.

She thought of his awful brother—she'd be fine giving *him* to the shade, but she never wanted to step foot in that house again.

"Well, you better go," he said, his gaze once again distant and bored. "The scorpion man is still out there, and there's only a few hours left before sunset."

Liliana nodded, there were still names left on the list. Julio, Ben ... Jeremy.

"Good luck," he said in her general direction before wandering off and disappearing between two buildings. *Where is he off to?*

She considered following him and turning her spy powers onto him instead but released the idea as quickly as she took hold of it. She turned and made her way to the parking lot. There were a surprising number of cars still in the lot, and for a second, Liliana didn't remember where she had parked. Shaken by what happened at Killian's house, she didn't pay attention to where she left her car when she returned to school.

She scanned the lot looking for her car, but what she saw instead made her heart pound and vision blur.

Jeremy was in the parking lot—he had Becca pressed up against his truck, his hands moving over her body as he kissed her.

21

Liliana's heart hammered and her eyes watered a little, her stomach twisting on itself. She felt like she was going to vomit. Instead, she just stood there, watching her boyfriend make out with the worst girl in school. *I thought Julio was giving her a ride home*, she thought dimly. She remembered watching Jeremy follow them; she thought he might have been going after Julio, but she was wrong. It was *Becca* he was going after.

She wondered why Becca hated her so much—now she knew why. *God, how stupid am I? How long ...*

Liliana thought back, trying to remember when Becca had started giving her a hard time. She closed her eyes and shook her head—all year. This had been going on *all year*.

Liliana couldn't believe she'd been so stupid. All this time she'd been practically skipping through life, so in love with her perfect boyfriend. Walking around campus holding hands, spending every free minute she had with him, all while he was sneaking around with *Becca*. She wondered who knew about this, who had been keeping this from her. Someone had to know, especially if they were doing things so publicly.

Liliana continued to watch them, willing Jeremy to stop, to turn, to see her. But he didn't—he kept kissing Becca.

"Hey, girl, what—" Helsie popped up beside her, her eyes following Liliana's gaze to where Jeremy and Becca were still entwined. "Oh, *Hell* no!" she yipped.

"In the *school parking lot*? How stupid is he?" Finn said as he threw an arm around Helsie's shoulders. Helsie glared at him and shrugged his arm off.

"What's *that* supposed to mean?"

Liliana didn't pull her gaze away from Jeremy as Helsie and Finn argued next to her. Their voices ebbed and flowed, and she couldn't focus on the words anymore. Everything she thought she knew about her life was wrong. *Everything.*

"Girl, you want me to kick her ass for you?" Helsie's voice broke through Liliana's thoughts, and she dragged her eyes from Jeremy to Helsie. With her curled blonde hair, full makeup, and petite frame, she looked like the last person who could kick someone's ass, but there was something wild flashing in her bright-blue eyes that made Liliana wonder.

"N-no," she managed to stammer. "Thanks, though." Liliana gave her a weak smile. She and Helsie weren't really friends, and Liliana often suspected Helsie didn't even remember her name since she always called her *girl*, but in that moment she loved her.

"Come on, Hels," Finn interjected. "It's none of our business."

Helsie gave Liliana a sympathetic look but let Finn lead her away to his own car. She always thought they were the most dysfunctional couple, but now …

Jeremy finally pulled away from Becca, and Liliana saw Becca see her. Their eyes held, and Liliana's pulse rocketed throughout her body, inside her head. She expected Becca to smile at her, to laugh, to pull Jeremy close for another kiss. But she didn't.

She stared back at Liliana, her face expressionless. Becca gave her a soft shrug, as if to say, *well, now you know.* Jeremy opened the truck door for her and Becca broke eye contact to jump into the passenger seat. He slammed the door with the quick flick of his wrist and turned. A light wind raked its fingers through his dark-blond hair, causing it to ripple like a wheat field. Even now she couldn't help but find him attractive.

He finally saw her, then. He froze and stared. She could practically see the gears turning in his head. He started toward her, moving quickly with long strides across the parking lot. As she watched him get closer and closer something fired up inside of her. Her frozen body released. She didn't want to talk to him. She looked desperately for her car, then saw it just a few down from where she stood. Liliana ran toward it, heart pounding. She needed to get inside the car. It was the only thought that consumed her as she ran. She needed a locked door between her and Jeremy.

Liliana unlocked the car and yanked her door open— but she was too slow. Jeremy's hand was around her arm, pulling her away from her car. He slammed the door shut with his other hand.

She whipped around to face him and yanked her arm out of his grasp. "Don't touch me!" she yelled.

"Shh, shut up, people are watching," he hissed angrily at her. Tears dribbled down her cheeks and blurred her vision. The last thing she cared about was who was watching.

"I don't know why you're acting like this," he said, a little more calmly as he ran a hand through his wind-tangled hair.

"You don't—" Liliana gaped at him. "I *saw* you!"

"What? What did you see?"

Liliana's eyes widened. "I saw you *kissing* her!"

Jeremy scoffed, a light laugh that made Liliana's blood rush faster through her veins.

"No you didn't, I'm just giving her a ride home. You're acting crazy."

For a brief moment Liliana called back the memory of what she saw. As she started to dissect it inside her mind it began to slowly fall apart—pieces crumbling away until she wasn't certain of what really happened. She'd thought she saw them kissing, but it was possible she just saw them standing close together and she jumped to the conclusion. She was experiencing a lot of crazy things, seeing things, hearing things. Was this just her mind messing with her? But Helsie and Finn saw them, too.

She hesitated, then noticed the peony-pink lipstick smeared on one side of his mouth.

"You have *lipstick* on your *face*, Jeremy!"

Jeremy's hand flew to his mouth and wiped at the greasy lipstick mark.

"*She* kissed *me*. I was just trying to be nice. I didn't want to hurt her feelings—"

Liliana shook her head. "You're such a liar."

She turned her back on him and opened her car door again, but again he shut it.

"You have no right to be angry, this is all your fault anyway." Liliana's head was spinning at the speed in which Jeremy changed tactics.

"You've been avoiding me, going to parties without me—you were probably making out with someone at that party while Diego was *dying*."

Liliana felt as if the air was punched out of her. *How could he say that?* She searched his face for the guy she had loved—for the guy who won her carnival stuffed animals, the guy who always reached to hold her hand. But the person in front of her was a stranger.

She forced herself to remain calm, forced herself to keep her hands down at her sides instead of slapping across his face. She thought of the fire balls again, this time relieved she *didn't* have that power. If she did, he'd be incinerated by now.

She wanted to hurt him, though, and there was only one way she could think of to do that. Liliana's head tilted to the side as she listened to Jeremy's death whisper.

Three years, four months, eight days.

The voice sounded like ... Liliana made a face. The voice sounded like vomiting. She wasn't sure what that meant, but she could guess.

She leaned in close to Jeremy, standing on her tiptoes to reach his ear.

"You're going to die alone," she whispered. "Choking on your own vomit."

"What?" he yelped, stepping back from her. "Is that some sort of threat?"

Liliana let a small smile curl her lips. "No. It's a fact."

Jeremy let her get into her car after that, a look of disgust and maybe fear on his face. She didn't watch him storm back to his truck. Didn't watch him speed out of the parking lot, Becca beside him.

Liliana sat inside her car and thought about the shade wrapped around Killian's neck. Telling Jeremy how he was going to die didn't bring her the satisfaction she thought it would. She wanted to *destroy* him. For cheating on her, for the awful thing he said about Diego, for making her feel like she was losing her mind. For how utterly *stupid* he made her feel.

Even if she did want to transfer the shade from Killian to Jeremy she had no idea *how* to do it. She pushed the shade and Jeremy out of her mind. Another thing she could let break her *later*—but not right now.

Right now, she had a different monster to find.

<h1 style="text-align:center">22</h1>

Instead of going home she drove straight to Julio's house—now that she knew Becca wasn't with him, she hoped to get another chance to talk to him. As she turned her car down his street, she sunk lower in her seat. Julio lived three houses down from Diego. She eyed her tía's house as she drove past. The house was unchanged from what it usually looked like, Diego's death so recent. The house she'd grown up in almost as much as her own now looked like some sort of movie set. A false calm around it, a mask hiding the grief inside.

The wake for Diego would probably start that night, or tomorrow. She would be expected to attend with her family, but she didn't know if she could do it. The thought of standing there with her entire family, pretending she didn't know what she knew. Pretending it wasn't her fault he was dead. *If I had just been faster, smarter...* she let the thought snuff out as she pulled up in front of Julio's house. She pushed her feelings down as far as they would go. She needed to focus.

Liliana parked her car but didn't get out right away, her hands shaking on the steering wheel. She felt so mixed up—like she was on a seesaw where one side was sadness and the other rage. She tried to gather herself; she couldn't go up to his door and burst out crying—or screaming.

Liliana got out of the car—she would just have to wing it.

She knocked tentatively on Julio's door. She had spent so much of her childhood in this house, playing with her cousin and his best friend. They liked to try and ditch her, sometimes playing hide-and-seek with her, but never bothering to seek when it was her turn to hide. She had fallen for that one more than once.

Julio's mother opened the door. She was short with a doughy body and her long graying brown hair woven into a neat braid down her back.

"*¡Ay, Liliana! Siento mucho tu pérdida. Comparto tu dolor, Diego era un buen chico.*" Liliana gasped as the woman pulled her into a tight, warm hug.

"*Gracias,*" Liliana replied as she searched her mind for the right words to say. "*Ha sido muy duro para mi familia. ¿Julio está aquí?*"

Julio's mother gave her an odd expression and hesitated before nodding toward the backyard. Liliana walked through the living room and let herself out through the sliding glass door and onto the back patio. Julio was sitting on a white bench swing, his arm wrapped around the shoulders of a girl with long, burgundy hair. Her face was buried in his chest.

Ruby?

Liliana watched, stunned, as Ruby bawled in Julio's arms. It was the second time in the last twenty minutes she'd seen two people together who shouldn't be. The sight of Jeremy and Becca together flashed before her, and she felt sick to her stomach again. She thought of Diego, who had never hurt anyone. Who had loved Ruby more than anything. The baseball team had replaced him—and now it looked like his girlfriend had, too.

Part of her knew that wasn't fair to Ruby. Part of her wanted to be mature and understanding. But that part of her was small and weak and easily squashed.

Julio glanced up and saw Liliana.

"Liliana!"

Ruby's head snapped up, and when she turned to look at Liliana, her eyes were red and wet. Julio leapt up as if the bench was on fire, leaving Ruby swinging alone.

"What are you doing here? Ruby just came over—"

"Don't." Liliana snapped, raising her hand up as if she could stop the words.

Ruby slipped off the swaying bench swing and stormed over to Liliana with tears in her eyes.

"Where have you been?" Ruby's voice cracked. Her long hair was messy and instead of her usually bright-colored clothing, she wore a loose-fitting black dress that fell to her ankles. She wasn't wearing any makeup—no sparkly eyeshadow, no deep red lipstick. She looked like a shadow version of herself, a ghost of who she once was.

"You haven't answered any of my calls or texts, you just left the party and then ... and then ..." Ruby's voice faded to a soft squeak as she began sobbing again.

Liliana took a step toward Ruby but she backed away. "Diego *died*, Liliana, my boyfriend is *dead* and you just disappeared!"

Something inside of Liliana snapped. Ruby had no idea what Liliana was going through, that she actually experienced Diego's death herself. Felt it. Seen it. Tried to stop it—and failed.

"He was *my cousin*, Ruby!" Liliana screeched back. "We grew up together, you think you're the only one hurting right now?"

Julio stepped between them with a desperate look on his face.

"Whoa, now, come on, it's a tragedy, we're *all* mourning—"

"Shut up!" Ruby and Liliana yelled at him in unison.

Julio threw his hands up in surrender and backed away toward the house. "I'mma let you two talk—"

"No," Liliana snapped. She couldn't let herself get sidetracked again. The sun would be down soon, she couldn't let Julio get away without learning something.

Liliana turned away from Ruby and stalked up to Julio, who was looking at her as if she were some sort of wild animal about to attack him. She stopped abruptly in front of him and stared into his eyes. They seemed human enough, his eyes. Deep brown, long dark eyelashes, warm. She listened to the death whisper wafting off of him.

Thirty years, five months, six days. The voice sounded like footsteps in the snow, breaking ice.

Liliana backed away from Julio. She couldn't be sure, not off just that, but it was hard for her to imagine a scorpion monster dying in the snow. It couldn't be Julio.

Behind her she could sense Ruby approaching, could hear the faint death whisper coming off her. *No, I don't want to know.* She shook her head to herself and dashed back into the house, leaving Julio and Ruby on the back patio.

Liliana rushed through the house and to the front door as quietly as she could to avoid drawing Julio's mother from the kitchen. Back in her car, she pulled out of the spot and drove until she found herself in a shopping center parking lot. She parked the car and tried to settle her ricocheting thoughts. Seeing Ruby at Julio's had thrown her. She assumed Julio had moved on from Ruby a long time ago, but seeing how he looked at her, how he held her, Liliana wasn't so sure.

She leaned her head back against the headrest and groaned. Everything was such a mess. She wished she had someone to turn to—but she'd pushed everyone away. Now someone else was going to die, and she didn't know who, or when, or—

Liliana's hands flew to her throat as she gasped for air, an ugly, hollow sound. It felt like her throat was caving in on itself and she couldn't breathe. She looked around frantically—there were plenty of cars around her, but she couldn't see any people. No one to help her. She panicked as she realized she was going to die—she was going to suffocate in her car in a shopping center parking lot.

How pathetic.

If she was going to die there, she wasn't going to go

quietly.

She opened her mouth and let out a long, painful scream before darkness overtook her.

23

Liliana opened her eyes but she could barely see—everything was a shadowy blur. She was in another body she couldn't control and this one seemed to need glasses. An empty ache pinched her stomach, like she hadn't eaten in days.

Liliana tried to pick up any clues that might help her figure out who she was inside this time, who she might be able to save. The light felt comfortable, dim, she guessed it must be dusk or dawn. She tried to focus on the body she was in, what she could feel, since she could barely see. She felt the warm pavement under her feet. *I must be barefoot. Why would I be barefoot in the street?*

She heard a choking sound come from a figure a short distance away. Liliana squinted—someone was standing on the sidewalk, but all she could make out was a blue-black blur. The body she was inside made its way slowly across the street towards the figure. With each step forward the person became clearer until she finally made out some features—long wavy dark hair, a heart-shaped face, short and curvy figure. Panic raced through her—she recognized the girl on the sidewalk.

It's me.

24

Liliana woke up with a jolt. It took her a second to realize where she was—still inside her car in the shopping center parking lot. She could breathe again, her throat open but sore. The light outside was dimming, and a glance at the car's clock told her an hour had passed since she pulled into the parking lot. She blanched at how much time she lost. The vision had felt so short; how could she have been asleep for so long?

The vision.

It was difficult to see anything clearly when she was inside that other body, but she'd been able to make out one thing—*herself.* Every body she'd been in had died shortly after her vision. Whoever she'd been inside was doomed to die, and she was doomed to watch it happen.

No. She shook her head. *If I'm not there, no one will die.*

She turned the key in the ignition and peeled out of the parking lot. She went through what she remembered from the vision in her mind as she drove home, but it wasn't much. Liliana was outside on a sidewalk, it was dusk—or dawn. She glanced at the cooling sky and chewed nervously on her bottom lip. *It's fine*, she told herself. All she had to do was get inside her house, lock herself in her room, and stay away from everyone until ...

Liliana let out a long breath. She had no idea for how long. She'd heard so many different death whispers, so many different time frames it could be.

Maybe I'll know, somehow, she thought hopefully. *My throat will stop hurting, or ...*

She stopped at a red light and groaned, her fingers tapping rapidly against the steering wheel. Liliana looked at the darkening sky and a surge of panic raced through her, up from her stomach, to her heart, to her hands.

Come on, come on!

After what felt like an eternity the light finally changed, but the car in front of her didn't move. She did something she never did—she punched the center of the steering wheel and a long, loud blaring sound blasted out. Through the back window she could see the person jump, then finally pull forward. Once she made it to the other side of the intersection she merged over and passed the slow car, then cut back in front of it. She'd never driven like this before, so aggressively, so angrily, but the fear of what lurked in her future fueled her forward.

I need to get home before the sun goes down. Please, just let me get home before—

Liliana took the turn onto her street a little too fast and gritted her teeth as the car tilted sideways, the right-side tires briefly leaving the ground before bouncing back down. She drove as fast as she could down her street, then slammed on the brakes. She lurched forward painfully, her seat belt cutting into her neck. There, in the middle of the street, in front of her house, was the ugliest creature she'd ever seen. And this wasn't the first time she'd seen it.

Its familiar, black-shelled body reflected a sickly yellow glow from a nearby streetlight as its eight hairy human arms gripped the pavement with strong fingers. Liliana felt hot vomit rush up her throat, but she forced it back down. The scorpion man wasn't looking at her—his attention was focused on someone else.

On the sidewalk just a couple yards away from the monster was her mother, long dark hair down and flowing, the three little Pomeranians at her feet barking wildly at the creature in the street. Her mother wasn't moving, just standing there, clutching the dogs' leashes and staring.

A cold realization flowed through her. She was wrong—it wasn't herself she'd seen in the vision—it was her *mother*. Which meant the body she'd been inside was ...

Something deep inside her told her what she had to do. What she was *destined* to do.

She slammed her foot down on the gas pedal and the car lurched forward, picking up more and more speed as she drove down her street toward the scorpion man. Neither of them noticed her coming, the creature's attention focused on her mother and her mother frozen stiff with fear. She braced herself as the car crashed into the scorpion man, her head flying forward and hitting the steering wheel painfully on impact.

Liliana would never forget the sound—a hard, wet slap against the car, then a rocky *thump, thump* as she drove over the body. She slammed her foot down on the brake after the second *thump*. Her hands gripped the steering wheel, but the rest of her body trembled uncontrollably.

Mamá!

Liliana clumsily pawed at the door handle, fighting with it for a moment before realizing her car was locked. She pushed the unlock button and half-spilled out of the car. Her legs were weak, fighting hard against gravity to keep her upright. She made her way slowly to the back of her car. She didn't want to see what was there, but she had to make sure it was dead. Had to make sure her mother—and everyone else—was safe.

But when she looked down at the body in the growing pool of blood it wasn't a scorpion monster she saw.

It was Ben.

<h1 style="text-align:center">25</h1>

Liliana stared down at Ben's broken body, his long dusty-brown hair matted to his face with blood. He was completely naked and his right arm and leg jutted out grotesquely at wrong angles. She'd wasted her time with Julio, with Finn. If she'd just been smarter, faster, maybe she could have gotten to him before ...

The body on the ground twitched and she took a startled step back. Ben made a pained gurgling sound in his throat, as if he were trying to speak. Tears slid down the sides of his face from his bloodshot eyes. He was still alive.

Oh, God.

She wanted to look away, but she couldn't. She stared down at the dying boy—the dying *monster*. Ben made the gurgling sound again then turned his head to the side and spat out a mouth full of blood. Bright red dribbled down the side of his cheek from the corner of his mouth.

"Thank you," Ben gasped out, his words wet with blood. "I'm s-sorr ..."

Liliana blinked at the boy she had run down with her car. The boy that had killed her cousin, his own girlfriend, maybe others. He would have killed her mother if she hadn't done what she had. She wanted to hate him, wanted to spit on his body, wanted to feel vindicated, but the way he looked at her—how his words had sounded. They made her feel hollow inside. He didn't have any choice. Just like she couldn't stop hearing people's deaths, he couldn't stop becoming the scorpion.

Ben's eyes closed and his body went limp. He let out a tiny gasp, and Liliana watched in awe as his spirit flowed from that last breath and took shape in front of her. Liliana squinted at the being floating over Ben's body. It was like looking at the reflection of a person in a steamed-up mirror. Just a foggy outline, a suggestion of a person. She blinked and it was gone.

The smell of fresh pine tinged with smoke filled her lungs and she coughed slightly, not needing to turn around to see who was behind her.

"He wasn't strong enough to control his own ancestry. Shame."

Liliana's mouth fell open at Mr. Reynard's callousness. Ben was more than the monster he was forced to become. He was a nice boy, he was in the marching band, he was planning on going to college, he loved Isabel. He had a whole life he had planned on having—a life that was now over. Because of *her*.

She felt soft arms wrap around her, recognized her mother's scent of sage and turpentine. The three little dogs were at her feet, whining and staring up at her with sharp black eyes. She turned in her mother's embrace to look at her. Her mother was unharmed, but her eyes were wide and wet, her lips trembling.

"What—what was that, what happened? You hit—that wasn't—who—"

Liliana hushed her mother and stroked her hair back from her tear-soaked face. "It's okay, Mami, it will be okay."

"You know it won't be," Mr. Reynard said, sliding his gaze away from Ben's body to look at her and her mother. His amber eyes were warm and caring but still full of ancient mischief. "All they will see is a kid you hit with your car—*on purpose.*"

"No," her mother said, grabbing Liliana's arm. "No, we all saw it—the monster, we can ..."

Her mother trailed off, her eyes wide and glistening. She shifted her gaze from Liliana to Reynard. "*No puedo perder a mi hija.* We can say it was an accident."

"He's right, Mami," Liliana said as soothingly as she could. "No one will believe us."

Her mother looked around the empty street frantically. "Someone must have been filming," she said, hysteria creeping into her voice. "Someone is always filming everything!"

The street was empty except for Mrs. Gyu, hunched over and mostly blind. She was inching along the sidewalk with her walker in front of her, yellow tennis balls on the ends. She looked completely oblivious to the bloody scene in the street.

Her mother shook her head fiercely and her nails dug painfully into Liliana's arm.

"Okay, no one saw. Okay. We will just say I was driving—"

"No, Mami!" Liliana wrapped her arms around her mom, tears starting to fill her eyes. "No, I won't let you do that, Mateo needs you—and Papa—"

"Violeta," Mr. Reynard interjected in a firm, commanding tone. He took her mother by the arm and gently extracted her from Liliana's embrace. Her mother looked up at him, confused. He smiled down at her warmly. "Why don't you go inside, lay down. *No te preocupes, yo cuidaré de tu hija.* I'll handle everything."

Her mother nodded, gripping Mr. Reynard's arm and gazing at him as if he'd solved all their problems. As if he was some sort of angel.

Liliana watched as her mother drifted up their driveway, the dogs' leashes clutched in one hand. The little balls of black fluff followed her obediently into the house.

"How—"

"I can be ... persuasive. Now, you have two choices," he said, facing her. She looked up at his smooth face and glowing amber eyes. "You can stay here and deal with the consequences," he gestured at Ben's bloodied body in the street, "or you can come with me."

"Come with you?" Liliana echoed. She slowly lowered herself to sit on the curb and rubbed at her aching head. She closed her eyes and in the darkness she felt a little calmer. She opened her eyes and looked up at Mr. Reynard suspiciously, wondering if he was working the same magic on her as he had her mother.

"It isn't a coincidence I happened to be your substitute teacher."

Liliana nodded to herself, only half-understanding.

"I came here for *you*, Liliana." He nodded toward Ben's broken body in the street. "I came for him, too. Alas, I wasn't able to get to him in time. But you, *you* I can still save. I can help you, Liliana."

"Save ...?" Liliana glared up at him. "Who are you, really?"

"Come with me and I'll tell you, I'll tell you everything you want to know. I'll take you to a safe place. Somewhere with others like you, where you can get a handle on your powers. They're only going to keep growing and you don't want them to overwhelm you." Mr. Reynard looked down at Ben again. "Ben was overwhelmed by his powers, and you see what happened to him."

Liliana looked away from Mr. Reynard, from the body on the ground. She glanced up at the dead walnut tree in her front yard, leafless branches graying and brittle. The crows were there again, staring down at her with their beady black eyes. Their feathers an oily bluish black.

"No, my abuela told me this is temporary—I am a descendant of La Llorona, that's why I—"

Mr. Reynard made an odd, choked sound deep in his throat. "Maria."

Liliana paled when she heard La Llorona's real name. She eyed the man suspiciously. "How do you know her name?"

"Maria is part of the reason I am here. She was a banshee. Had always been a banshee, deep down. When her powers awoke she didn't understand them. They drove her insane ... and she killed herself and her children and became nothing more than a sad folktale." The man shook his head and looked up at the sky. For a second she thought she saw the shimmer of tears in the dimming light. But when he looked back at her his eyes were dry.

"What does that mean?" Liliana asked, her voice

strained. "This is never going away? I'll have to listen to people's deaths, *see* people's deaths, for the rest of my life?" Liliana shook her head, her own eyes starting to water. Mr. Reynard said nothing for a moment, just looked at her as if he were waiting for something.

"I tried to help Maria, but ..."

He looked away for a moment, then back to her. There was a seriousness in his eyes she hadn't seen before. "I tried to help her, but she refused to listen to me. Liliana you must know—this is just the beginning, it's going to get much worse. Don't make the same mistake she did."

Liliana looked up at the strange man she barely knew. She studied his pained expression, the pleading in his eyes. His words echoed what he had written in that note to her. *It's going to get worse.*

"I can't—I can't leave my family," she replied, her voice breaking. "And I have plans ... I'm going to college ...."

Even as the words left her mouth she knew she was lying to herself. She wasn't going to college, not anymore. The life she'd worked so hard to build, the life she'd dreamed of, was gone before it had even begun.

Liliana's head spun and she felt like she was on the verge of hyperventilating. The words Mr. Reynard said ricocheted around her head too fast for her to hold on to. She couldn't make sense of any of it, and all she wanted to do was to go to her room and hide under the covers. Close her eyes tightly until the vision of Ben was erased from her memory. Until *all* of it was erased from her memory.

"I don't mean to rush you, but I can't keep all this hidden much longer, it's tiring."

Liliana looked down the empty street and realized she hadn't seen anyone since Mrs. Gyu went into her house.

"Hidden?"

"Of course, you think all of this would go unnoticed?" He scoffed, the softness he'd just shown her gone. "Once I let go the world will start back up again, there will be onlookers, police, questions. You need to decide—are you coming with me?"

Liliana gazed down the empty street, the street she grew up on. The street she learned to ride a bike on, the street she had her first kiss. The street she thought would always be here for her. She had wanted to leave, wanted to be on her own. But not like this—she'd always thought she'd be able to come back.

She scrutinized the mysterious man, his perpetually laughing eyes, his deep red hair. She barely knew him, and yet she was considering going with him to some unknown place. She imagined, for a moment, what would happen if she stayed. She would call the police, say it was an accident. Tell them that Ben had just ... run in front of her car. She nodded to herself. It was believable. He was naked, that would help. It'd look like he'd just gone crazy and ran naked in front of her car. It would be difficult, but in the end she'd be released. She'd be fine.

She let her gaze fall back onto Ben. He hadn't been able to control his powers—his ancestry. She swallowed tightly when it occurred to her that he'd had his powers a lot longer than she had. His birthday was over a month ago. Her heart pounded harder in her chest as she unraveled the thought. All of this had only started a few days ago—which meant ... it meant he was able to control it at first, and then one day he couldn't. She thought of Maria, who let the voices drive her insane.

"What—what do you mean it will get worse? What is going to happen to me?"

Mr. Reynard crossed his arms and looked more like the substitute teacher he'd been pretending to be.

"Your powers are just now awakening, the omens and shades are just now taking notice of you." He nodded up at the crows still watching them from the dead walnut tree. "Your powers will grow, will change, and worse things will start to notice you. If you can't control your powers, can't control the omens and shades ..."

Liliana pulled her knees to her chin and wrapped her arms around herself tightly. She didn't want to admit it to Mr. Reynard—or herself—but she knew. She was barely keeping it together now. Liliana didn't know if she would be able to handle much more. She didn't want to end up like Maria and Ben.

"Okay," she said softly. "I'll go with you."

She forced herself to stand on shaky legs and turned to look at her house. The house she'd grown up in, the house she'd planned to return to for visits from college. A college she was no longer going to.

Her father wasn't home from work yet, her brother was probably in his room. She had no idea what her mother was doing. She ached thinking of Mateo, of the awful story he would be told about her. She'd be a murderer—a murderer who *ran*. Liliana couldn't leave him without saying goodbye. Without trying to explain why she was leaving.

"I'll be right back," she said and ran up to her house before Mr. Reynard could object.

Inside her mother was sitting at the dining table with a steaming cup of tea in front of her. She was staring down at the cup, her eyes red from crying. She didn't look up as Liliana passed through the room.

Liliana stopped in front of Mateo's bedroom door, she could hear him playing one of his video games. She hesitated, then kept walking to her own room. *Not yet.*

In her bedroom she quickly filled a duffle bag with a random assortment of things. Underwear, sweaters, T-shirts, pants. She had no idea where she was going, or how long she would be there for ... she stuffed as much as she could into the bag. Liliana hesitated when she saw the turquoise choker necklace Jeremy gave her, a small puddle of blue stones on her desk. She picked it up and threw it in her small trash can and continued packing.

When she couldn't fit any more things in the bag she zipped it up and took one last look around her room, a hot ache blooming in her chest. She looked up at the ceiling where the little glow-in-the-dark star stickers were starting to glow faintly in the darkening room. She jumped up onto her bed and reached up to peel one of the stickers off the ceiling. She tucked it into her pocket and hopped off the bed, grabbing her heavy duffle bag and leaving her bedroom for what felt like the last time.

She made her way back to Mateo's room, this time pushing through the door before she could lose her nerve.

"Hey!" Mateo yelled from his navy-blue beanbag chair on the floor. "You have to knock!"

Liliana set her duffle bag down on the floor and took a deep breath to ease the tightness in her chest. Mateo's anger faded when he saw the bag.

"What's that?" he asked, pushing a button on his controller to pause the game.

Liliana squatted down next to her little brother and tried not to cry.

"Mateo, I have to leave, and I don't know if I'll ever be able to come back." She choked out the words, her eyes ignoring orders and spilling tears down her cheeks. "I'm sorry, I don't want to go."

"What are you talking about?" he asked slowly. "Why?"

Liliana took a deep breath in an attempt to calm herself, in an attempt to keep from completely losing it there on the floor in her brother's room.

"It's complicated ... but ... you're going to hear things about me. Bad things. I'm not sure what Mamá will remember once I'm gone, she's ... not herself right now. I just want you to know, you know, that I love you and I—"

"*¡Basta!*" Mateo snapped, shaking his head furiously. "Just stop it."

Liliana sniffled and tried to rub the wetness off her face. Mateo stared at her, his deep brown eyes serious, almost commanding. She stood up and ruffled his hair one last time. He didn't jerk away.

She picked up her bag from the floor and hesitated in the doorway. Mateo looked liked he was slowly sinking deeper into the beanbag chair, his body growing smaller as she watched. She could hear Mateo's death whisper but refused to listen to it. She couldn't bear knowing.

"Goodbye, Mateo."

She stopped briefly in the kitchen, her mother was still staring down at her teacup, no longer steaming but still full. Liliana walked over and kissed her mother's damp cheek. "*Te quiero, Mamá. Lo lamento.*"

Her mother's eyes remained downcast, like she was lost inside of herself. Liliana looked down at the three Pomeranians at her mother's feet.

"Take care of her."

The dogs each tilted their head and Liliana took that for agreement.

Outside Mr. Reynard was waiting for her on the sidewalk and part of her wanted to change her mind. Wanted to run back into the house and hide from all of this. But she couldn't.

Liliana took one last look at her home. She didn't get the chance to say goodbye to her father. She almost asked if they could find him first but thought better of it. She wasn't sure she could handle another goodbye.

She nodded to Mr. Reynard.

The tall man with deep red hair and preppy clothes took a few steps toward her and then disappeared. In his place stood a large red fox with familiar amber eyes.

The Teumessian fox.

He walked closely around her in a circle as his long fire-red tail wrapped around her legs. She felt the brush of soft fur on her bare skin, and then she felt nothing at all.

26

Ava let out a soft growl as she watched her best friend disappear with the red-haired substitute teacher. She knew something was off about him; he didn't smell human, and by now Ava was *very* familiar with the scent of humans. She backed deeper into the tall grasses, forcing the sharp spikes along her spine to lay down. There was a bitter taste in her mouth. She didn't have a chance to say goodbye—and Liliana didn't hesitate before leaving with a stranger.

"She's in danger," a matter-of-fact male voice said from beside her. She flinched and the spikes along her spine stood straight up again. A man she didn't know stood beside her, had gotten *this close* to her without her realizing it. She sniffed the air—he didn't smell human, either. He smelled ... *wrong*. Like a fresh sea breeze but with a hint of rotting seaweed.

In her other body, she might have been afraid to find herself alone in the dark with a strange man, but not in *this* one. In her chupacabra body, she was simply angry she'd been caught off guard.

She let her long, black tongue run suggestively across the razor-sharp fangs she bared at him. He looked young, with a swimmer's body and shaggy blond hair. He had a casual, airy vibe that didn't mesh with the seriousness of his words. She had never killed a human before, but he wasn't human. He was something else. Something that might make a tasty snack.

"She won't be coming back," the man continued. Ava could not speak in this body, but she responded by letting out a breathy *huff*. The man didn't seem to notice, but continued to stare straight ahead at the spot where Liliana and the teacher had just been.

"The man she left with—the fox. He was *made* to trick people. To cause chaos, ruin. She's not safe with him."

Ava growled softly, the two hearts inside of her beating out of rhythm. She tried to keep Liliana safe, but she had failed. She had let him *take* her.

Ava knew immediately when Liliana had changed. Her scent was human one day and something else the next. But it was a smell she wasn't familiar with, a smell of blood and river water. It had scared her, that first day. She still didn't know what Liliana became.

"Why don't you come with me?" the man said, breaking through her thoughts. "I can help you—I can help you help *her*."

Ava looked down at the blood-soaked street where Ben's body still lay. Where just a moment ago Liliana stood with the teacher. She tilted her large head, squinted her yellow reptilian eyes at the man.

"It won't be easy, saving her," the man maintained, unbothered by Ava's complete lack of response. "But we must. She's important."

Ava's two hearts pounded in her chest and her long tail flicked angrily back and forth behind her. She hated herself for letting this happen. Hated herself for letting Liliana think she was alone.

Ava went through her own change over a month ago, on her eighteenth birthday. The first time it happened she was driving home from her birthday party. It felt like she was being stretched in a hundred directions, pain flaming through her veins. Her hands and feet became webbed and clawed, her skin gray and leathery, and six sharp spikes grew down her spine. Ava lost control of her car and crashed it into a towering saguaro on the median. She ran off into the night, abandoning the car, her phone, and in a way, herself.

She woke at dawn the next day in her own backyard, naked and covered in blood that wasn't hers. She still didn't know how she kept it together that morning, how she sneaked into her house and cleaned up before her dad and stepmom found her. Her father screamed at her for what felt like hours for crashing her car and fleeing the scene. When he asked her what happened, she told them she swerved to avoid hitting a hare. Crashing her car because of her love of animals was a lot easier to believe than "I transformed into some sort of monster."

She learned to control it after that. She had to feed every few days, usually on goats and other farm animals, but she chose when she became the chupacabra.

Ava wanted to tell Liliana what had happened to her—what she became. But there was no way Liliana would believe her friend became a hideous half-coyote, half-lizard abomination. Still, she could have told her, *should* have told her, after she had sensed Liliana's change. Things might have gone differently—but instead here she was, forced to watch as a man she didn't know stole her away. Liliana was forced to trust a stranger because Ava didn't trust her with her own secret. She eyed the man next to her as her long black claws dug into the dry dirt. She hated being forced into a corner. Hated being left with no choice at all.

"Come now," he said gently as he turned away from Ava. "And I will explain everything."

27

Liliana stared out across a long pond at the impressive manor on the other side. The duffle bag of things she'd packed weighed down one shoulder and her skin goosebumped from the sudden damp coldness of the lush forest she found herself in.

It was late, wherever she was, the sky velvety dark with the only light coming from a few of the manor's windows. The impressive structure looked like it belonged in the Deep South, with antebellum architecture complete with Grecian pillars and romantic arches. It was painted white, with two stories and a wraparound porch. French double doors cut the house perfectly in half. The second floor had a deck that reflected the porch, wrapping across the front of the house. Vines with tiny, pale-pink blooms grew up the pillars, braiding themselves around the bars of the wraparound balcony. A few of the windows were lit up, but most of them were dark. A small bridge stretched across the pond just a few feet away from where she stood.

"Welcome to your new home," Mr. Reynard said, a soft purr on the back of her neck.

She turned to look at him. "What is this place? Where are we?"

"It's a safe place, hidden from the human world. It's a place where you'll be able to learn to control your powers without interference."

Liliana squinted at Mr. Reynard, confused. "What do you mean, 'human world'?"

"It's a long, complicated story, one I do not have the time to tell you at the moment." He turned and began walking away from her, then paused. He must have sensed her frustration because he turned back towards her with a sigh.

"This world looked very different before humans arrived and took over. The witches transformed magical beings—the ones that couldn't hide themselves, at least—into humans to protect them from, well, humans. Every three hundred and eighteen years the descendants of these beings are ... reminded, I suppose you could say. Of what they really are. Last time this occurred ... there was a lot of chaos. A lot of death. I swore that I would do better the next time the descendants awoke. I have taken it upon myself to help these creatures any way I can. Like I helped you."

"I don't understand. What about my mother, my grandmother? Abuela said they both got powers on their birthdays but the powers went away. They aren't both over 300 years old."

Mr. Reynard nodded. "Yes, it is unusual. Your family line must be very strong for a glimmer of power to appear in that way. But as you said, their powers didn't last long. Your only equal is Maria."

He turned away from her again. "I won't be here much, I must find the others and bring them to safety. As we speak, a mermaid is waking, and I must go to her."

Liliana's eyes widened. *A mermaid?* She'd been so wrapped up in herself, in her own dark powers, she hadn't thought of what other creatures might be out there. For the first time excitement bubbled up inside her chest. She was obsessed with mermaids when she was a kid. Now she was going to actually meet one!

"Now go, get some rest. It's been a hard day for you."

It was true, Liliana felt completely drained. In the last three days she lost everything—her family, her friends, her boyfriend, her future, her *life*. She was exhausted to her bones, to her soul.

"Vaira and Kai can show you around and get you ... acclimated. I hope to return in a few days."

Liliana perked up at the mention of other people. *Other people* was a good thing. Though the manor had some of its lights on, she had imagined an echoey, empty building.

"Go ahead inside, they're expecting you."

Expecting me?

Liliana hesitated. She struggled to understand how anyone could be expecting her— everything happened so quickly. She slowly took a step toward the small bridge that arched over the pond and led to the other side where the manor waited.

"One thing, it's dangerous for you out there," Mr. Reynard added. "This place is safe, but what is beyond the tree line is not. Please, do not venture into the woods."

Liliana turned to ask a hundred questions, but he was already gone.

She eyed the surrounding woods and shivered. There was a dampness to the air and the scent of wet leaves and pine surrounded her. The last thing she wanted to do was venture into the dark, cold forest by herself.

She turned back to the manor, the lights inside beckoned to her and she took a step up onto the cute, if rickety, bridge that arched over the pond. As she walked across the bridge, she admired the moon-bright water lilies floating on the calm surface of the water. Jewel-bodied dragonflies flitted from bloom to bloom and she thought she saw the shadows of fish moving under the surface.

As she stepped off the bridge the manor loomed large above her, and she felt much more intimidated than she had when she saw it from across the pond. Her heart was beating painfully fast and her chest ached. She took a deep breath and held it, then let it out slowly. *This is your life now*, she told herself fiercely.

Liliana approached the impressive French doors and raised a trembling fist in the air, then let it slam down against the wood—once, twice, three times.

Next in the
Forgotten Legends
Series

Feathers
&
Fortunes

Coming Fall 2024

www.ingramcontent.com/pod-product-compliance
Lightning Source LLC
Chambersburg PA
CBHW021154310726

48971CB00002B/634